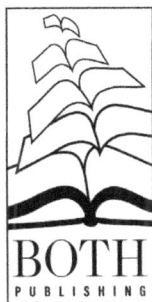

BOTH
PUBLISHING

Originally published in 2015
by Harper Collins *Publishers*.

This edition published in 2025
by BOTH Publishing.

A CIP catalogue record of this book is available
from the British Library

ISBN - 9781913603472

Printed by Ingram Spark.
Distributed by BOTH Publishing.

Cover design, artwork and typeset
by Chrissey Harrison.

Part of the Dyslexic Friendly Quick Reads Project.

www.booksonthehill.co.uk

The Beach Cabin

Fern Britton

Other dyslexic friendly quick read titles from BOTH publishing

The Necessary Arthur

Stamp of a Criminal

Sharpe's Skirmish

Sherlock Holmes and the Four Kings of Sweden

Silver for Silence

Anchor Point

The Breath

Ultrasound Shadow

The Man Who Would Be King

A Scandal in Bohemia

The
Beach Cabin

Prologue

Channel 7 Studios, London, 2000

The floor manager of *Skool's Out*, Channel 7's hit children's TV show, watched the action play out in front of him in a state of high anxiety, rather like a budgerigar left in charge of a cattery, never sure from which direction the danger was going to come from. The programme always went out live at 5.15 p.m. on a Friday and the whole operation was a test of nerves, patience, forbearance and arse-licking for the entire crew. Despite the old show-business adage about never working with animals or children, the set was always filled with dozens of hysterical pre-teens, plus that week's line-up of novelty acts. This typically consisted of an assortment of pet dogs that could whine the National Anthem, a nine-year-old who could fart at the same decibel level as a car horn and some idiot intent on breaking a silly world record, like how many times you can kick your own butt in one minute. On top of this the crew had to contend with the fragile egos and sometimes ridiculous demands of the celebrity guests, combined with the inflated ones of the show's presenters. Anything could go wrong, and it was a fine balance between giving the show's trademark anarchy full flight while keeping things under control.

The set was designed to look like a school where the kids had taken over. Walls were daubed in graffiti, there were 'detention' cells that the guests could be placed in if they displeased the 'kids' and everything had a slightly sinister quality that was pitched somewhere between St Trinian's and a Tim Burton movie.

The floor manager heard the director's voice from the control room through his earpiece. "Dave and cameras move over to the cell area for Robbie's detention skit."

"Yep." On the set, Robbie Williams had been placed in one of the cells and was being lambasted by the show's irreverent star, a puppet called Brian the Cat – a mass of tatty black-and-white fur and Denis Healey eyebrows who spoke in the thick Mancunian tones of his puppeteer. Brian was lambasting Robbie from outside his cell accompanied by his sidekick, a young presenter called Kirsty.

"Robbie Williams, the studio audience have unanimously decided to give you detention on account of not only crimes against…"

The audience howled with laughter.

"…but also, for eating all the pies!"

Cue more hysterical screaming.

Ed Appleby, the studio runner, watched tensely from his position behind the camera crew. He could see Robbie's PA and his publicity manager watching stony-faced from the wings. If things went too far and Robbie got upset, there would be hell to pay. Ed took his *Joe 90* glasses off, gave them a quick wipe before putting them back on and then ran his hand anxiously through his dark curly hair.

Brian the Cat was egging the audience on. "What do you reckon? Shall we let him go home now, kids? Has he done his detention?"

"Splat him!" the children screamed. Robbie grabbed the cell bars and shook his head vigorously, mouthing something Ed couldn't hear over the roaring of the audience, but which looked suspiciously like, *Bollocks to that*.

"Let him have it!" declared Brian triumphantly, and a bucket that had been hovering above Robbie's head tipped over and released a yellow goo over his head.

"Camera one, zoom in," said the director over talkback.

The camera zoomed in to see Robbie's expression as the yellow gunk slicked down his face and chest.

Robbie wiped the gunk away from his eyes with his fingers and licked his lips. There was an anxious pause in the room before Robbie said in his soft Northern accent, "Mmmn, lemon curd, nice. Can I have a jar to take back to me mam, sir?"

As the audience cheered their raucous approval, Ed saw the faces of Robbie's people relax.

The camera moved away to Kirsty. "Ha-ha! Now let's see the new video from

5ive – they're going to be here next week and we're going to give them a proper *Skool's Out* welcome, aren't we?"

Ed's shoulders relaxed briefly, but they immediately tensed again as he felt someone sidle up to him and gently pinch his bottom. He turned sharply and was immensely relieved to see Charlotte Finney, the show's design director, standing next to him. They were virtually the same age, but, while Ed was still working his way up the ranks as a lowly junior, Charlotte was responsible not only for the way the show looked, but also the tone and feel. All the senior managers took her seriously, though, judging from her expression, she was feeling anything but serious. She gave him a cheeky wink.

"Thank God it's you!"

"Who else were you expecting to make contact with your sexy arse, Ed?" she said huskily.

"God knows in this madhouse," he whispered back. "I'd better go."

There would now be a brief three-minute video interlude for everyone to get to their new place, make a quick costume change and prepare for the next segment.

Ed shot Charlotte a look that said *sorry* and raced over to release Robbie from his temporary cell. A posse of Robbie's people and studio assistants followed hot on his heels, bringing hot towels and clean clothes for the star. Declining their offers of help, Robbie took off his T-shirt and used it to wipe away

8

the yellow slime while flaunting his taut and tanned six-pack.

"Keith, you fucker, I'll get you back for that!" he said good-naturedly to Brian's puppeteer, Keith Puckley, who had extricated himself from Brian's undercarriage.

"Didn't they tell you at stage school that this would happen, Rob?" Brian shot back.

"Fuck off!" Robbie grinned, and playfully poked Keith's middle-aged paunch. "Who ate all the pies, eh? I think we know the answer to that one!"

"Must mean I'm in with a chance as your replacement in Take That – give your mate Gary Barlow a call and tell him I'm free."

Before they could trade further insults, Ed interjected: "Keith, you're not free yet – Brian has to judge the burping competition in one minute. Robbie, we need to get you cleaned up for the finale. You're singing us out with 'Rock DJ'."

"Oh yeah, ace." With a final grin at Keith, Robbie headed off to make-up, entourage of flunkies in tow.

Ed and Keith looked at each other. Only another thirty agonising minutes to go, then they could all breathe out.

An hour and a half later, Robbie had been dispatched in his limo, the kids had all been loaded on the coaches that would take them home to Milton Keynes or wherever it was they had come from, and Ed was sitting on the steps at the rear entrance of Channel 7's Soho studios, smoking a crafty cigarette. The doors behind him opened with a crash as Keith, still accompanied by Brian the Cat, emerged. The puppet was operated from below with a combination of levers and sticks, which allowed his limbs to function. Brian's head and body lolled lifeless over Keith's arm.

"Thank fuck that's over for another week," said Keith with feeling as he plonked himself down on the step next to Ed. "I'm getting too old for all this shit."

"Rubbish," said Ed. "The show wouldn't work without Brian. You love it, you know you do."

Keith grunted something unintelligible

in reply, lighting up his cigarette and pulling heavily on it.

The back door opened again and Charlotte stepped out. He wasn't aware of it, but Ed's face lit up as if it had been illuminated by a thousand-watt light bulb. Charlotte was dressed in green army combat trousers and a fitted black T-shirt that showed just a hint of her soft creamy belly when she lifted her arms up. Her choppy, layered red hair, probably a shade of red that didn't occur in nature, framed her oval face and made her green eyes greener. Charlotte had told Ed that she was actually a blonde, but he didn't care. He thought she was utterly gorgeous.

"Keith Puckley, put that cigarette out now!" She pointed at Keith accusingly. "If

Brian gets a fag burn it'll be Muggins here that'll have to sit up all night stitching him, or, God forbid, making another one from scratch – which I've already had to do once, thanks to the Christmas party shenanigans."

"Sorry, Charlotte," said Keith meekly. "I was gasping."

"Oh, all right, but be careful." Charlotte softened and ruffled Brian's fur affectionately. "God knows why, but I've become attached to the horrible little bastard."

"You wouldn't want to be as attached to him as I am. Feel like I can't get away from the little bugger," he said gloomily.

Charlotte patted his arm sympathetically. "Maybe it's time to put Brian back in his box, Keith. It's been a long day."

"You're probably right." Keith stubbed out his cigarette and stood up. "Time to go home."

As he departed he said, "And no getting up to any hanky-panky, you two. I might be an old duffer but I don't miss much."

Ed and Charlotte tried to look innocent. "I don't what you mean, Keith," Charlotte said, trying to stop a grin from spreading over her face.

"A likely story." He wished them goodnight and headed inside.

After a moment, once she was sure he'd gone, Charlotte inched closer to Ed so that their thighs were touching. Her hand crept under the back of his T-shirt and she leaned in to nibble his ear.

Ed's senses felt under assault; she smelled of fresh meadow flowers and Ed could feel the swell of her breasts against his chest. It took all his willpower not to reach under her T-shirt and slip his hand under her bra. Despite this, it was Ed who pulled away first.

"We'd better be careful, someone might see us."

Charlotte slipped her hand into his. "They all know already.

Look at Keith – and he's well out of the gossip loop."

"No." Ed shock his head. "They don't know. Not officially, anyway, and I don't think they should, not yet. We've talked about this."

She pulled away and looked at him

with a frown. "Yes, we might have talked about it, but I still don't see we have anything to hide."

Ed squeezed her hand and tried to make light of it. "I know you don't, but you're the design director and I'm the lowly runner.

They'll think I'm trying to sleep my way to the top." He tried to engage her with a smile.

Charlotte's frown deepened. "I don't care what they think. We've been seeing each other for nearly a year. Your toothbrush can't remember what your bathroom looks like, I let your best friend sleep on my sofa for three weeks and I've played in a Scrabble contest with your mum. For heaven's sake, Ed, we couldn't be more together if we tried."

"But you know what the top brass are like. They hate relation- ships on set in case things go wrong."

"What's going to go wrong?" Charlotte looked alarmed.

"Nothing! Nothing's going to go wrong, Charlotte. But I'm building my career, and yours is going so well. We don't want anything to spoil that, do we?"

Ed felt as though the conversation was running away from him but couldn't work out where he'd gone wrong. This was the first time Charlotte had ever said anything about wanting their relationship to be more open. They'd both been happy for their work and personal lives to be separate – hadn't they?

He pulled his cigarettes from his top pocket, took one for himself and offered one to Charlotte. She shook her head, her lips set in a thin line.

"I've given up."

"Since when?"

"This morning."

"Oh?"

Ed removed the cigarette from his mouth unlit. Charlotte was looking at him, an unreadable expression on her face. It wasn't a look he recognised or that he felt particularly comfortable with, if he was honest.

"What's wrong, Charlotte?"

Charlotte tugged at her long fringe, something he'd noticed she did when she was nervous or anxious.

"Something's happened."

When he thought about it later, Ed realised what she said next was literally the last thing he'd have thought she was going to say. He'd have been less surprised if she'd told him she'd been born with a penis and had undergone a sex change.

"I'm pregnant."

That she uttered these words and not some others was his justification for his response, though he knew as soon as the words left his mouth that it was completely the wrong thing to say in the circumstances.

"Oh, shit!"

Charlotte immediately stiffened, eyed him with a look that seemed to communicate both disappointment and distress, and snatched her hand away from his.

"Oh, shit!" he said again, unable to absorb what those two words could mean for both of them. Registering the look in her eyes, he panicked. "I didn't mean oh, shit, I meant oh, no. I mean, it's the timing, isn't it, for both of us." Unable to stop himself, he blathered on: "Your job, mine... I always thought we'd get together properly one day – you know, married, kids and all that – but just not now..."

This was all coming out wrong. He looked at Charlotte, his secret girlfriend... beautiful, clever Charlotte... the mother of his children...

At this thought, a little spark seemed to ignite somewhere inside him and for a moment he saw them, his future family, and words and feelings that he'd never recognised in himself flickered within him: father, husband, protector...

But Charlotte was getting up off the step, moving towards the door. She reached for the handle, then paused to look back at him. "The traditional response when someone announces they're expecting a baby is 'Congratulations!' Look, we'll talk about it later, Ed. You're right, my timing is shit."

"Wait, Charlotte!" He leapt up and reached for her, but she brushed his hand away.

"Look, Ed, it's fine. We'll talk later. Right now I need to go home."

As Ed watched her retreating back and scrabbled to his feet to catch her, he knew he'd screwed it up big time. If this was a test, then he had failed miserably.

He only hoped it wasn't too late and she'd give him a chance to make things right.

1

Pendruggan, Cornwall, 2015

Penny Leighton was sitting in the kitchen of the Old Vicarage with her feet up on the kitchen table – it was her table, after all – enjoying a freshly poured cup of tea. For once the house was quiet: her husband had gone over to the church hall, where he was hosting the Pendruggan Mother and Toddlers' Group as part of his vicarly duties. Across the table, Ed Appleby hunched over a laptop, wrinkling his brow as he perused stately homes on his web browser.

"That list Cassie sent over of possible locations for Lady Arundell's family pile – I've worked my way through and eliminated the ones that wouldn't be suitable. Lanhydrock would be ideal, but I also like the sound of Prideaux Place, smaller but gorgeous. It's not far from here and apparently it has amazing grounds overlooking Padstow. As we've got a break in filming, maybe I should arrange a meeting with the owners, do a recce – what do you think, Pen?"

When his question went unanswered, Ed looked over the top of his laptop. The producer of *The Mr Tibbs Mysteries* seemed oblivious to his presence. She had just dunked a HobNob in her tea before popping it into her mouth and was currently savouring the soft, sugary crunch. A look of sheer bliss on her face, she let out a long "mmmm".

Ed took off his thick-rimmed Michael Caine glasses and rubbed at his tired eyes. "Did you hear any of that, Pen?"

"You know, without your glasses on you look about seventeen." Penny dunked another corner of her biscuit into her tea.

"Don't change the subject."

"Why not? Why do we have to talk about work? We've four weeks' enforced break while our leading lady goes off and does her one-woman thing at the Old Vic. What's wrong with spending a morning eating HobNobs and taking it easy for once?" She cast a longing gaze at the copy of *Grazia* lying unopened by her side.

Mr Tibbs, based on the novels of Mavis Carew and filmed on location in the picturesque Cornish seaside village where Penny had made her home, had proved to be such a runaway success that they were now halfway through filming the fourth series. The invasion of the cast and crew, and the transformation of Pendruggan into something straight out of the 1930s, had become an annual fixture in the village calendar. Some of the locals had been resistant, but most welcomed the film crew, especially now that the series had put Pendruggan on the tourist map. Queenie's shop had become a must-see destination for the holidaymakers who flooded the village each summer.

Ed sighed and shut his laptop.

"Besides," Penny added, "it's not your job to sort out locations. Cassie's already done half the work. Let *her* go and see them. She's more than capable. You can make your decision once she's written up her recommendations."

"I'm the location manager. It's my job."

"Cassie's the assistant location manager, and that makes it *her* job. It's called delegating, Ed. Anyway, you look exhausted."

"I am exhausted."

"Then go home and try to put your feet up for a while. Spend some time with Charlotte and those gorgeous children of yours. You all look like something out of a Boden advert."

Ed let out a humourless laugh. "Looks can be deceptive, Pen."

Penny put down her cuppa and leaned closer.

"What's the matter, Ed? You and I have worked on umpteen productions together over the years. I've seen you go from junior runner on *Blue Peter* to location manager on a Woody Allen movie, and, no matter how demanding the job, you've shown up for work full of enthusiasm and energy. I've never seen you out of sorts – until now. You're usually so cheerful – *too* bloody cheerful, in fact!"

"But it hasn't affected my work?" he asked anxiously. "Has anyone said anything?"

"No of course not. Don't be silly." She batted away his anxiety with a wave of her hand. "No one's noticed a thing. Except me, and that's only because we've known each other such a long time."

Ed wiped his glasses clean on the corner of his SuperDry T-shirt and let out a sigh.

"Oh, I don't know ..." He hesitated, wondering how to articulate what he was feeling without making it sound melodramatic? "Alex has been a bit difficult lately. She's not been herself and Charlotte's worried something's up at school."

"She's fifteen," Penny reasoned. "They're unknowable at that age. You and Charlotte are there for her, though. You're solid, right?"

Solid, thought Ed. Before all this had happened he wouldn't have hesitated to say yes. They both adored the kids and put their needs first. For Ed that involved taking on work that meant they could leave London and buy a large house on the seafront in Worthing, and cover school fees so that both kids got the best education possible, plus a bit left over for long summer holidays in the South of France so they could spend time as a family. For Charlotte it had meant giving up work until the kids started school. Then she had become involved with a local theatre group, helping out with set design – always fitting it around the children's needs, because Ed wasn't around to help as much as he would like. In order to command the big salary he had to spend large chunks of time away on location. The last couple of years, he seemed to have spent most of his time at the opposite end of the country to Charlotte and the kids.

"I think so," he replied, trying hard to keep the uncertainty out of his voice. "Charlotte says I'm away too much."

"Are you?"

"Perhaps, but only the last year or so. You know how it is in this business, Pen. Projects are tied up years ahead, you sign your life away."

"You're one of the best in the business, Ed. You can pick and choose your projects now."

"I'm not so sure. People have short memories."

"Only for people they want to forget."

Ed laughed at this. "Point taken."

But the thing that was really worrying him was the one thing he couldn't bring himself to tell Penny. Over the past year the distance between him and Charlotte had been growing, and it was a distance that had nothing to do with being at opposite ends of the country. They always used to make the most of the weeks when he was at home, but now Charlotte seemed to spend every minute she could at the theatre. Worse still, she'd taken to sleeping in the spare room, citing his fidgeting in bed as the reason. "I've got used to sleeping without you, Ed," she'd told him bluntly.

Ed felt sure there was more to it. Whatever their ups and downs over the years, the two of them had always been physically close. It made this new distance between them all the more painful. Then four weeks ago, during his last stay at home, he'd waited until Charlotte had gone to take a bath before sneaking into the spare bedroom and picking up her phone. Though he hated himself for it, he clicked on her inbox and scrolled through the messages. Among them he found one that made his heart stop. It was a text message from Henry, the director at the theatre. He could hardly bear to think about the words he'd seen: *I love you… can't live without you…*

The thought that his wife was in love with someone else tore at his insides. He pushed it away.

"Look," said Penny, pulling him back to the present, "what you need is a break. Why don't you bring them all down here for the weekend? One of the cottages in the village is for rent. It's recently been bought by some second-homers who're letting it out when they aren't here. It would be perfect for you and the family, and the best thing about it is that it's got this amazing beach cabin on Shellsand Bay that comes as part of the package."

"How do you know it's available?"

"Queenie told me. The owners have engaged her as their key holder. I can easily get their number off her." Penny picked up her phone and started to call Queenie.

"Hang on, I'm not sure. I'd need to check with Charlotte – they might have plans."

"Ed, stop procrastinating. You need to spend some time with your family and that's that."

Ed did as he was told. Now that the idea was in his head he ached to see his kids. The last four weeks he'd avoided going home, citing complications with the production. Anything rather than confront the situation and risk Charlotte telling him that she no longer loved him, their marriage was over.

Maybe Penny was right. They hadn't been seeing enough of each other, that was all. He'd been letting his imagination run riot. Yes, they could sort this all out – a little holiday was exactly what they needed.

🐚

"Please can you get off my foot, Molly?" Charlotte looked down into the soft adoring eyes of their bearded collie. Molly was a shaggy-coated four-year-old, absolutely enormous and intent on getting as close as she could to Charlotte, which meant that crushed toes were part and parcel of being a dog owner in the Appleby household.

Charlotte eyed the ingredients in front of her. Prawns in their shells. Coconut milk. Now what else was it that Nigel Slater had said should go in? The recipe had been in the *Observer* at the weekend, but she'd forgotten to tear it out before chucking the paper into the recycling box. She'd decided to give it a go anyway, hoping that she could rely on her memory. A green curry – would that be Indian? Or Sri Lankan? She rummaged in the cupboard and fished out some curry powder. What else? There'd been a green herb of some sort... And was it a lemon or a lime he used? She went to the fridge: there was no lime, so it would have to be lemon, and the only green herb she could see was a slightly withered stalk of parsley. That'd do. Maybe chuck in a carrot or two? And mangetout – she had plenty of mangetout and it was definitely one of Nigel's ingredients.

Any other evening Charlotte would have abandoned all thought of making the dish as soon as she discovered the recipe was lost, but tonight she was glad of the challenge. She needed something to distract her from the worries racing through her mind. Alex should have been home an hour ago. They'd agreed that she could go to her best friend Poppy's house for the afternoon, provided she was home by seven. When seven thirty rolled around with no sign of her daughter and no word of explanation, Charlotte had tried to ring her, but an automated announcement informed her that the person she was calling was not available. So she rang Poppy's mum to ask her to send Alex on her way – only to discover that Alex hadn't been there in days. Fighting the urge to panic and ring all three emergency services and run up and down the street in hysteria, she'd focused on remaining calm and waiting it out. It wasn't the first time Alex had disappeared for a few hours with no explanation. It had been less obvious during term time, though Charlotte had managed to catch her out a few times, but now the holidays were here it was clear that Alex was going somewhere she didn't want anyone else to know about.

There had been none of the usual telltale signs of a boyfriend. No dreamy looks over the breakfast table, or furtive late-night phone calls. Charlotte wasn't much of a snoop, so she could be wrong, but in her experience boy trouble usually came with bells on, shouting its presence loud and clear. No, this felt like something else. Perhaps if she'd been around a bit more, then Alex would have opened up to her. But she'd been preoccupied with everything that was happening with Henry – she'd be lying to herself if she didn't admit taking her eye off the ball.

Charlotte proceeded to chop up all the ingredients with more confidence than she felt. The resulting mix looked nowhere near as lovely as the photos of Nigel's efforts...

She lit the flame under the deep sauté pan and threw in the vegetables. Behind her she heard the front door shut quietly in the hallway and turned with great relief to see her daughter Alex slipping past the kitchen door in the direction of the stairs.

"Hi, darling," she called out.

Alex's foot stopped on the stairs.

"Hi, Mum."

"Got a minute?"

Silence, but then, a moment later, the slow plod of reluctant footsteps back down the hall. Alex's hair had been purple when she'd first dyed it, but it had now faded to a lilacy-blue and was scraped back in a ponytail. Charlotte missed her daughter's natural copper-blonde hair but hoped it would stage a return one day. Chewing the toggle of her hoodie, Alex hovered by the door.

"Been somewhere nice?" Charlotte asked casually. *Must avoid an argument*, she told herself. *Tread carefully.*

"I was at Poppy's, I told you."

Damn. Why do you have to lie, Alex? Why can't you tell me where you've been?

"I'm making dinner. Are you hungry?" she asked, a touch too brightly.

"No, thanks. We had KFC."

We? Who's 'we'?

"What is it?"

Good question. "It's a prawn curry. Nigel Slater."

Alex rolled her eyes. "Why don't you just stick to ready meals, Mum?"

"I like cooking." It was true.

"But you're not very good at it."

"I shall ignore your implied insult. I've been complimented on my cooking, I'll have you know."

"Only by Granny Alice, who lost her taste buds when a bomb fell on her house during the war."

"Not only Granny Alice, actually: many people."

"Yeah, right, Mum," Alex replied sceptically, turning to leave.

Charlotte was on the verge of letting her go, but then decided it was time to bite the bullet and confront her daughter. "Alex, I called Poppy's mum when you were late home. She said—"

Alex's explosive response took Charlotte by surprise, even though she'd been exposed to enough teen anger that she ought to be used to it by now. "How dare you! You're always snooping around and following me. Why can't you let me live my own life?"

"Alex, darling, I don't want to interfere, but you're only fifteen and we worry about your safety, that's all."

43

"Rubbish! You just want to control me."

Charlotte struggled to keep her voice even. "Alex, I understand how—"

"No, you don't! You can never know how it feels to be me!" And, with this, Alex raced out of the room and up the stairs, slamming her bedroom door behind her.

Charlotte looked at Molly, who was cowering under the pine kitchen table. "Well, that went as well as can be expected," she muttered, and Molly crept out and sat on her foot again, giving her hand a consoling lick. "Thanks, Molly. I can always rely on you to be here for me."

If only she could say the same of her husband. Charlotte silently cursed Ed for never being home when he was needed. Instead, he was hundreds of miles away as usual while she held the fort at home, though it felt very much like a battle she was fast losing.

He was so much better with Alex than she was; he always knew how to bring her round. Part of the problem was that she and Alex were too much alike: spiky, emotional rather than rational, prone to keeping secrets... But the old Alex had hated confrontation. On the rare occasions when she did get in an argument, she was always the one who would try to make up. The familiar gnawing guilt fluttered in her belly, berating her. *This is your fault. If you weren't spending so much time at the theatre... All that time with Henry when you should be at home...*

As if on cue, her phone rang. It was Ed. *Hello, stranger*, she thought.

"Hi, Ed. How's it going?"

"Yeah, good. We're finished now for four weeks – Dahlia's gone off to do her one-woman show in London."

"Oh, God, that! What's it about again?"

"Um, not sure – something to do with older people having a lot of sex?"

"Crikey."

"Kids OK?"

"You probably know better than I do."

Whenever he was away, Ed kept in daily contact with them by text and FaceTime.

There was a pause at the other end of the line. She could picture him floundering over what to say next without putting his foot in it.

"I was wondering," he said eventually, "how would it be if you all came down to Pendruggan for a few days? There's a great place we can stay – it's right by the beach. We haven't seen much of each other over the last few weeks—"

"Months, more like. And whose fault is that?" Charlotte couldn't stop the words slipping out.

"I know, I know." Ed's voice sounded pained. "But I think it would be good for the kids – and for us."

"I'm not sure, Ed." Charlotte knew from experience what a holiday could be like when Ed was in work mode. "You couldn't find time to join us in

France last month. Apart from one long weekend when you deigned to make an appearance, I had to hold the fort with my mum and dad. And those few days you *were* there you spent on your laptop or iPad, working. And when you weren't working you were sleeping – or drinking too much."

There was silence from the other end of the line. Charlotte was already regretting her outburst and was on the verge of apologising and explaining why she'd felt the need to vent when Ed suddenly blurted, "Please, Charlotte, I promise I'll be totally 'there'. No phones, no laptop, no iPad. Just us. We need this."

Charlotte breathed in deeply. "Let me think about it and call you back.

Alex is being tricky at the moment, and, even at the best of times, getting the kids to do anything outside their comfort zone is practically impossible. Besides, Pendruggan is a good five-hour drive, and—"

"It'll be worth it," Ed pleaded. "I promise you – come on, let's do it."

Still Charlotte wouldn't cave in. Promising that she'd call him back once she'd spoken to the kids, she hung up the phone and eyed the contents of the saucepan. It hadn't looked like this in the *Observer*. She pulled the ring on the tin of coconut milk and hoped for the best.

Charlotte knocked on Sam's door and popped her head in. Her eleven-year-old was sprawled across his bed watching a YouTube video on his iPad.

"Dinnertime."

"What is it?" he asked, without looking up.

Charlotte looked down at the gloopy rice-and-sauce concoction on the tray she had brought up. "Prawn surprise."

Sam raised his head and frowned at her. "Is a prawn something you want to be surprised by?"

"That's a very good question, Sam. Perhaps we're about to find out the answer."

She sat next to him on the bed and he scrutinised the contents of the tray.

Taking the beaker of milk, he took a long slurp and said, "Can I have a burger in a bun?"

Charlotte looked down sadly at the prawn surprise. "Would Birds Eye be an acceptable option for you, sir?"

"Perfectly splendid, m'dear." And Sam finished off the milk and replaced the beaker on the tray with a flourish.

"What's that you're watching?" Charlotte asked.

"This is the most amazing thing ever, Mum. It's Spike Turner, the skateboard pro. He's doing this totally awesome bitchslap."

"Sam!"

"Don't be lame, Mum – it's skate lingo." For the next five minutes Sam gave her an incomprehensible commentary that consisted of terms like *nollie*, *lipslide* and *mongo*. She tried to keep up but most of it went over her head.

"Sam," she ventured when at last there was a brief lull in his analysis, "how would you feel about a little trip?"

"Where to?"

A voice behind them said, "Cornwall. To see Dad."

They both turned to see Alex standing in Sam's doorway holding her phone. "I talked to him already – he called to tell me about it."

That was crafty, thought Charlotte. As always, he'd managed to get Alex on side. The mood she was in earlier, it must have taken a major charm offensive to win her over.

"So, what do you think?"

"I want to go. I haven't seen Dad for ages."

Charlotte looked at Sam. "What about you?"

Sam barely glanced away from Spike's latest heelflip. "Dunno. Have they got Wi-Fi?"

"Yes," said Alex. "I checked that with Dad."

"Cool," said Sam. "Then I can show Dad Spike's video."

Feeling that she was losing control of the decision-making process, Charlotte chimed in: "Hang on a minute. There's no way I'm going to drive all the way to Cornwall for the weekend so that the pair of you can sit watching YouTube or texting your friends the whole time. I want us to do things as a family, otherwise we might as well stay here."

The children both shrugged. "OK," they said in unison.

"It's a bloody long drive, too, so we'll have to be up and ready to go by six a.m. And I'm not doing all the packing by myself – you'll both have to help."

"OK."

"And we have to make it a proper break, be a family, do things together."

"OK!"

"Even if it means not being glued to your iPad for the next three days?"

"OK! OK!"

As Charlotte scraped the untouched prawn surprise into Molly's bowl she wondered at the ease with which the children had agreed to come. Maybe this trip was something that needed to happen. If nothing else, it would give her and Ed a chance to have a proper talk, clear the air. They'd been dancing around each other for too long.

As Molly sniffed noncommittally at her bowl, Charlotte picked up her phone. She'd text Ed later. First she needed to call Henry...

2

It was gone 9.30 a.m. and Charlotte was only now switching on the satnav.

"Mum!" whined Sam from the back seat. "Why does it have to be me in the back with Molly?"

"I've told you, Sam, you can swap seats with Alex halfway through. Now let me concentrate on putting this postcode in the satnav so we can get going. I was hoping to miss the worst of the traffic, but we're so late—"

"It was you who overslept, Mum," Alex pointed out smugly.

Charlotte cast an irritated glance at her daughter, sitting in the passenger seat fiddling with her headphones.

"That's because I was up past midnight, packing."

"You love your bed too much, Mum."

"It *is* the holidays." Charlotte wasn't sure why she needed to justify herself. She and the children were all good sleepers. It was Ed who tossed and turned, often padding downstairs in the middle of the night, dogged with insomnia brought on by worries about work.

"Mum!" Sam nudged the back of her seat with his knee. "Why do I have to get stuck with Molly?"

Charlotte turned to look at Molly. The expression 'hangdog' could have been coined especially for her. Molly's head was hung low and her soulful eyes gazed out mournfully from under her shaggy hair.

"Poor old Mol," Charlotte cooed sympathetically. "You totally hate car travel, don't you, girl?" And she reached out to stroke her. Molly responded by giving her hand a sorrowful lick, then put her head down on her paws with a sigh.

"Nobody gave her any food, did they?" Charlotte asked suspiciously.

"No," they both answered, but Charlotte thought that Sam looked shifty.

"Sam?"

"Nothing, I promise!" he protested.

"Well, if Molly gets sick," she warned,

"I'll have a pretty good idea why. Now, let's get this show on the road."

"Hang on, Mum," Alex said suddenly, rummaging in her bag. "I've forgotten my charger."

"Alex!"

"What! You were rushing me!"

"Oh, just hurry up, will you." She thrust the door key at Alex, who leapt from the car and ran towards the house. Shaking her head, Charlotte returned her gaze to the satnav, which had just finished calibrating. The estimated journey time popped up on screen: five hours and seven minutes. *Great*, thought Charlotte, *this is going to be so much fun*.

Adjusting the rear-view mirror, Charlotte caught sight of herself and pushed her long fringe behind her ear. Her short, layered hairstyle hadn't changed much over the years, though the spicy copper colour was a thing of the past. Charlotte's naturally light-blonde hair was now flecked with grey, which she disguised with highlights. The smattering of freckles over her nose and cheeks gave her a girlish appearance, but there was no ignoring the crow's feet and laughter lines that were becoming more prominent with every passing year. It didn't bother her unduly: getting older was better than the alternative, she always thought.

Alex dashed back to the car and thrust the door keys at her mother. "Did you lock up?"

"Yes."

"Double-locked it?"

"Yes, Mum. Let's go!"

"Right, A303, here we come. Oh, by the way, we're going to make a little stop en route…"

♦

"Where are we going, Mum?"

Two hours in and Alex had finally taken off her headphones. Sam was dozing on the back seat.

"Well…" Charlotte said enthusiastically, "I thought we'd stop at Stonehenge."

"Why?"

"It's sort of on the way, and you and Sam have never seen it, and I haven't been there for years. And… why not? We're on holiday, aren't we? We said we'd do things as a family – and you promised there'd be no grumbling."

"Don't remember promising that," Sam mumbled under his breath from the back.

"It's a bit random, Mum." Alex raised her eyes heavenward.

"No, it isn't." Charlotte was conscious of the defensive tone in her voice. She was wondering now what had possessed her. As much for her own benefit as the children's, she tried to explain why she felt the need to make this detour: "Stonehenge is an amazing place. I came here when I was a kid, but couldn't remember anything about it, so I asked your dad to bring me here once when it was the summer solstice. I was pregnant with you at the time."

"Really?" Alex sounded genuinely interested for once.

"Yep. So, technically, you've been here too."

"Cool."

Charlotte stole a glance at her daughter. Alex had Ed's nose and his eyes and his brown wavy hair. Sam took after her with his fair hair and skin.

"What were you listening to? On your phone?"

Alex shrugged. "One of my Spotify playlists."

"Oh, like those ones that you and Poppy used to spend hours putting together in the kitchen?"

"It's not one of those," Alex said tetchily.

"Oh." It suddenly struck Charlotte that she couldn't remember the last time Poppy had been round to the house. The two girls had been best friends ever since primary school and had made the leap to senior school together. For years they'd been inseparable, wearing the same clothes, liking the same films and music and TV shows, and even sounding alike. But, apart from Alex telling Charlotte that she'd been with Poppy when she hadn't, there'd been no mention of her for ages. Charlotte could have kicked herself for not realising that Poppy hadn't been on the scene for a while. Perhaps she'd give Carol, Poppy's mum, a call and ask her about it, though Alex would go nuts if she found out she was snooping.

"Stick it on the Bluetooth and let's have a listen? I could do with waking up. So could Rip Van Winkle back there." Charlotte nodded towards Sam in the back seat. "We'll be at Stonehenge soon."

Alex paused as if weighing her options, then gave another shrug and connected her phone to the Bluetooth. A moment later a playlist popped up on the screen of the car's media player: 'Lily's Love List'. The first track came through the speakers, it was 'Stay with Me' by Sam Smith.

"Who's Lily?" Charlotte asked.

Alex stiffened. "No one."

"No one called Lily?"

"She's just one of the girls at school," Alex said through gritted teeth.

Clearly, the question had hit a raw nerve, but Charlotte had no idea why. Who was this girl? And, if the two of them were friendly enough to be sharing playlists, why hadn't Alex brought her home?

Charlotte put the questions to one side for a moment as she sang along with Sam's lonesome sentiments, but, the moment she did, Alex clicked on her phone and stopped the track.

"'Why did you turn it off? I was enjoying that."

"You were ruining it! Can't you put your Happy Mondays CD on like you normally do."

All right all right, thought Charlotte, *don't get your knickers in a twist.* She popped the CD in. The last thing she wanted was to infuriate her touchy daughter even further.

The car pulled up on the roadside and the three of them looked at the 4,500-year-old monument. A light rain was falling and the ancient site sat behind a wire fence, cloaked in drizzle. Charlotte couldn't help thinking that they weren't seeing the place at its best.

"What do you think? Hordes of slaves dragged those stones across the country to get them here, you know."

There was a moment's silence before Alex said, "It's smaller than I thought it would be."

"Yeah, it's puny," Sam agreed.

"It's quite big, actually. It's just that people have these preconceptions…"

"Yes," Sam said flatly. "Preconceptions that it's bigger and better than it actually is."

Charlotte tutted at his lack of appreciation. "Well, the last time I came—"

"*We* came," corrected Alex.

"The last time *we* came it was amazing," she persevered.

Charlotte could remember the day so vividly. She'd been eaten up with anxiety. Her pregnancy had been going well, she was fit and healthy and her midwife was pleased with how things were progressing, yet she couldn't help feeling overwhelmed at what was to come. She decided that what she needed was something to ground her, something to remind her that childbirth was part of the endless cycle of life and not merely something to scare the shit out of you. She'd always liked to dabble in alternative stuff. Ed used to tease her about it, saying she was a bit 'woo-woo', but she didn't care. A lot of it was mumbo-jumbo, but you couldn't argue with the magical antiquity of a place like Stonehenge.

The summer solstice was approaching and she'd told Ed that she wanted to see the sun rise at Stonehenge, never expecting that he would embrace the idea. But he surprised her by offering to drive them there, and he'd even booked them into a B&B somewhere close the night before so she wouldn't be too tired to appreciate it. As they ate a pub meal on the eve of the longest day of the year, Charlotte could hear the locals discussing the approaching event.

"Only them druids is all that's allowed on the site now," said an ancient barfly as he supped his pint.

Curious, as they got up to leave Charlotte asked him whether they would be allowed to join the ceremony.

"No, my love, they don't let anyone 'cept druids come to the stones these days. Too many New Age travellers and the like spoiling the site, they reckon."

Charlotte was bitterly disappointed that she wouldn't be able to get close enough to touch the stones and feel the connection between herself and the baby growing inside her with something timeless, enduring and powerful.

But, at 4 a.m., Ed had woken her gently and told her to wrap up in warm clothes. She didn't know how he'd found out about it, but he drove them a little way from the site and they walked through something called Stonehenge Avenue. He told her that this was the ceremonial route to the ancient site and that they were walking in the footsteps of their Neolithic ancestors. He spread his waterproof coat out for them to sit beneath a row of beech trees. And, as the sun rose over Salisbury Plain, Charlotte was left speechless by the breathtaking spectacle of the summer solstice taking place below them. It was beyond words.

As she peered through the drizzle now, Charlotte couldn't help but reflect the difference in her feelings then and now. She couldn't imagine Ed doing anything that spontaneous these days. Everything he did was planned and plotted down to the minutest detail. She sighed. What on earth had happened to them?

Her thoughts were interrupted by Sam's groan from the back seat. "Mum, this is so boring! Who cares about a load of old ruins? It's raining and it's my turn to sit in the front!"

"You're right," she said, peering out gloomily through the windscreen at the procession of tourists trudging around the fence. Resignedly, she waited for the children to swap seats. "Pass me a sandwich from that M&S bag." She took a bite, started the car and pointed it towards Cornwall.

They arrived in Pendruggan three hours later. Apart from a false alarm when Alex had shouted that Molly was hanging her head in that funny way she did before she got carsick and they had to make an emergency stop, the journey was uneventful. Alex was in a world of her own, plugged into her headphones, while Sam kept up a constant prattle on the subject of Spike Turner and Casper flips and pop shove-its and nosegrinds. Charlotte was pretty good at tuning him out when she needed to, though she couldn't help feeling that Sam deserved a more receptive audience – and, if his father could only be bothered to be a more available dad, he'd have one.

They all cheered when the sea finally came into view. By this time the weather had brightened considerably and Charlotte was heartened by the sight of the sparkling blue expanse. She loved the sea, and it always had the power to make her feel good. Everything was better by the sea, wasn't it?

As they entered Pendruggan, she was thrilled to see that it was a typical Cornish village with rows of robust cottages rendered in local stone, their doors painted in bright seaside colours. Some of them had lifebuoys and upturned lobster pots and nets lying in their front gardens. Charlotte wound down the window so they could hear the loud cries of the gulls that circled above.

In the centre of the village was a green, and around it she could see that all the needs of the villagers could be met: there was a shop, a church with what looked like a beautiful vicarage close by; there was even a red telephone box that actually seemed to have a working phone inside it.

Her satnav directed her to a turning that led to a row of cottages.

She drove carefully up the gravel track.

"Look at that cute one, Mum." Alex pointed at an extremely pretty cottage called Gull's Cry. They drove to the end and Charlotte felt her heart lurch when she saw Ed standing outside what must be their holiday let. It had been over four weeks since they had last set eyes on each other – the longest they'd ever been apart. Even when he'd been filming abroad, they'd always managed to slot some family time into the schedule, with Ed flying home or the rest of them flying out to visit him on location.

She pulled up in front of the cottage; there was no driveway, just a small front garden filled to bursting with lavender, rosemary, hebe and other scented shrubs. Alex was the first out of the car and she threw herself at her father, who hugged her back tightly.

Sam was close behind, chattering excitedly as his father rubbed his hair and slung an arm around his shoulders. Determined not to be left out, Molly bounced around Ed's legs, yapping excitedly.

Ed waved to Charlotte, waiting for her to join them before ushering the children inside. She was aware that she was taking an age to park the car. Her insides tightened again and she took a deep breath to steady herself, knowing that this flutter of nerves was a precursor to the conversation that she and her husband needed to have.

"What do you think?" asked Ed, eager for her approval. It seemed to him that the cottage was every bit as perfect as Penny had said it would be. The front door opened straight into a small but perfectly formed living room with a wood burner in the fireplace. It was snug and cosy, with comfy sofas and cushions strewn around, though it had probably taken a lot of hard work on the part of the owners to make it look so casually thrown together. Through the back was a kitchen that had everything a family on holiday could need, and dotted around everywhere were pictures of boats and the sea.

"It's amazing, Ed," Charlotte agreed, and Ed felt himself breathe a sigh of relief. He'd been on tenterhooks for hours, wondering what she'd make of it.

They trailed after the children as they raced up the stairs to check out the bedrooms, with Molly bringing up the rear. There was a double with an en-suite and two single bedrooms, plus a bathroom.

"This one's mine!" joked Sam about the master bedroom.

"You'll be lucky." Ed ruffled his son's hair.

The children bickered good-naturedly over their rooms as Charlotte checked out the en-suite bathroom.

She ran her finger along the side of the antique Victorian bath. "They've thought of everything, haven't they?" she said, clearly impressed.

"The owners have only recently put it on the rental market and it's getting towards the end of the season, otherwise we wouldn't have got a look-in." Ed sat down on the edge of the bath and pulled his wife towards him. "I think this is big enough for two, don't you?"

Charlotte gave a little shake of her head, but held his gaze. "Looks small to me." Then she deftly slipped away from his embrace and headed back out to the hallway, entreating the children not to let Molly jump on the bed.

Ed's heart sank. The look in his wife's eyes was guarded, distant, but he cautioned himself not to rush things. It was always like this after a big job away; they needed to find their way to each other again; get the first row out of the way and the first night in bed together – whichever came first, hopefully the latter – then get back to normal. *Be patient… Give her some space*, said the voice in his head.

Putting on a bright smile, he went to join the others, who were now admiring the view from Sam's designated bedroom.

"What do you think that is?" Sam was pointing to a shedlike structure in a large garden beyond.

"Penny said it belonged to someone called Tony. Apparently it's a shepherd's hut."

"Is he a shepherd, then? I can't see any sheep."

Ed tried to recall what Penny had told him about the man who lived there, but it eluded him for the moment. "I'm sure they must be around somewhere," he said vaguely. "Anyway, the tour's not over yet – and the best is yet to come!" He couldn't keep the bubble of excitement out of his voice; this was the part he had been looking forward to most.

Charlotte eyed him curiously. "Oh?"

"Come on." He slipped his arm around Charlotte's waist and ushered her to the stairs. "We're going for a little walk and you are going to love what we find at the end of it…"

It was by now late afternoon and the sun was starting to sink towards the horizon. As Ed set off with his family in tow, heading past the church and down a path that led to the sea, they could hear the sound of the waves getting closer, and the unmistakable smell of the sea filled their senses.

As they rounded the headland, Ed heard Charlotte gasp as she took in the view.

"Oh, Ed, it's beautiful!"

"It's called Shellsand Bay."

Below them a gentle path led down the side of the cliffs to the most beautiful beach. The late sun cast its rays on the clear blue water set against a cloudless azure Cornish sky. Ed had been desperate for the weather to be perfect for their arrival; he wanted everything to be just right. Knowing how much Charlotte loved the sea, he turned to see whether Shellsand had had the desired effect. Even after fifteen years together, the sight of her took his breath away. Her green eyes looked bluer with the sky reflected in them, and the gentle breeze ruffled her fair hair.

"I love it," she said simply, drinking in the colours and the rolling cliffs as they tumbled towards the golden sands.

"I thought you would." He smiled as he took her hand. "But there's more to come. Follow me."

At the bottom of the path, as the beach opened up in front of them, Ed pointed towards a small row of beach huts. "Look."

There were about half a dozen of them, all painted in primary colours. One or two looked as though they could use some love and attention, with faded paint and rusty hinges, but Ed led them to a bright-red hut that had obviously been well cared for. A Cornish flag fluttered from the roof. There was a step up to a small veranda outside the padlocked entrance. Ed took the step, brandishing the key. "It's ours!"

Alex shrieked, her teenage 'whatever' face momentarily forgotten. "Seriously, Dad, this is awesome!"

"Come on, Dad, let's have a look inside," Sam urged, leaping onto the veranda.

Ed put the key the padlock and had to wriggle it around for a moment before it turned.

"Hurry up!" urged Sam, jumping up and down with impatience. "Keep your hair on!" Ed turned the handle and at last the door creaked open.

The interior of the cabin was more spacious than it looked from the outside.

"Cool. It's like the TARDIS in here," observed Sam.

There was an old fifties kitchen dresser in the corner. Charlotte opened the doors: it was full of mismatched crockery. There was a tin tea caddy filled with teabags and little pots containing sugar, instant coffee and lots of other useful things. A kettle sat on one of the shelves and there was a sixties Formica-topped table with two chairs. In the corner, propped up against the wall, were deckchairs, a windbreak, a barbecue and all sorts of other beach paraphernalia. Sam was beside himself when he found a surfboard and a trunk containing wetsuits and snorkels.

"Dad, we've got to try these!"

Ed wasn't so sure. "They look a tad snug," he said cautiously. "They might not fit..."

"Dad, they're made of rubber – they'll stretch. Besides, you're thin as a stick insect." Sam made a stretchy-rubber face.

"Well, let's think about it, shall we?" Ed had never been surfing and didn't consider himself to be very athletic. Hopefully, Sam would be distracted by something else before he was called upon to deliver on that front.

"What do you think of it, Charlotte?"

Charlotte, who was lovingly fingering the bleached wood on the veranda and gazing out at the rolling surf, turned to him, her eyes shining joyfully. "I don't know what to say. I never expected anything like this."

Ed stood beside her and put his arm around her shoulder, gently pulling her towards him. She didn't resist, and a moment later her arm found its way around his waist. He'd forgotten how good she felt.

"It's an amazing place, Ed. I can't believe you've never brought us here before."

"This is the first time we've ever had a break in the schedule. Usually I'm so busy the whole time I'm down here, I don't venture far off the set. I never really thought of it as a holiday place."

Ed felt Charlotte's hand drop away from him. He looked down at her face.

She gazed out steadily towards the horizon, but said nothing.

"What are you thinking?"

She was silent for a moment and he held his breath, waiting. "Nothing." She turned to him and smiled, her smile reaching her eyes for the first time since she'd arrived. "Nothing. I'm so happy to be here, Ed. It's perfect."

And Ed found himself hoping that this would turn out to be true.

3

Ed was so disorientated when he
awoke that it took him a moment to
remember where he was. He fumbled
for his glasses at the side of the bed,
then set about looking for his watch.
His mother had given it to him after his
father died; despite a few scratches and
knocks, it had served him well. It wasn't
a particularly expensive watch – just
a stainless-steel Accurist with a mesh
strap – but Ed thought it was quite cool

in a seventies sort of way. It kept his dad close, though he'd been dead now for over twenty years; cut down in his prime by cancer.

He was stunned to see it was 9.30. How had he managed to sleep in so late? Even when he was at home, he was normally an early riser, so attuned to the hours of a filming schedule that he didn't need an alarm clock. He must have been more tired than he realised.

It took a moment for it to sink in that the bed beside him was empty.

The previous evening, they'd driven to the nearest town, Trevay. It was a typical Cornish seaside resort and the queue outside the Fairy Codmother fish-and-chip shop snaked down the seafront. They sat on the harbour wall with their food on their laps, the children happily chucking chips to the aggressively hovering seagulls while Molly looked on incredulously as she was denied even one – Charlotte was always pretty strict about not rewarding dogs who begged. Ed waited until she wasn't looking before giving Molly his leftovers, then they returned to the cottage and he opened a bottle of wine. He'd sipped from a glass while trying unsuccessfully to light the wood burner, while behind him Alex and Sam argued about what movie to watch on Netflix.

"You decide, Charlotte," Ed suggested. "*The Wedding Singer* or *Ghostbusters*?"

"*Ghostbusters*, obviously."

"Mum!" Alex protested. "We've seen it a million times already."

"Don't drag me into it, then. I'm going to hit the hay anyway."

"You're not going to stay and watch?" Ed was disappointed, he was hoping that they could have a cuddle on the sofa – get closer again – but Charlotte insisted she was too exhausted after the long drive.

"I can hardly keep my eyes open. Don't let the kids stay up too late. Night, you two."

Ed watched her as she kissed the tops of the children's heads, then made her way up the stairs. Just before the bedroom door closed, her voice drifted down: "Don't drink all of that bottle to yourself or you won't be able to sleep."

The kids drifted off to their rooms before the end of the film and, by the time he had tidied up and made it to bed himself, Charlotte was in a deep slumber, curled up in a foetus position on the far side of the bed. She might as well be on the far side of the world, he thought glumly as he climbed under the covers, wishing the gulf between them would disappear.

Now, he swung his legs over the bed and padded across to the en-suite bathroom. On the way he caught sight of his naked torso in the large mirror that hung over the dresser. He stopped for moment to study his reflection; he'd never had to worry about putting weight on. He seemed to have hollow legs – 'nervous energy', Charlotte called it – but he thought he could see a creeping tyre around his middle. He jabbed at it, trying

to remember when he'd last exercised.
A few years ago he'd taken up running
as a way of getting rid of some of that
excess energy so that he could get
a good night's sleep, but over recent
months he'd felt so drained and lacking
in motivation that he'd abandoned his
daily run. Perhaps that was why he was
sleeping so badly.

He slipped on his jogging bottoms
and yesterday's T-shirt and headed
downstairs. The staircase was narrow
and the wooden steps felt cold beneath
his feet.

He was surprised to see Sam already
awake and engrossed in his iPad.
"Morning, Sam. Where is everyone?" He
plonked himself down on the sofa next to
his son.

"Mum's taken Molly for a walk and Alex's still in bed."

"What you looking at?"

"Spike Turner."

"Who's Spike Turner?"

Sam rolled his eyes and tutted. "Dad! He's the world number-one skate pro and, like, the most awesome dude, like, ever."

"Right. I see." Though he didn't. "What's he doing?"

"Honestly, Dad, do I have to explain everything?" Sam pointed to the screen. "Watch this!"

Ed watched as a man of about thirty-five in a baseball cap, baggy jeans and a SuperDry T-shirt skated towards a flight of steps, launched himself on his skateboard and coasted down the handrail, before flipping his board 360 degrees, executing a perfect backflip and then landing on his board.

"Wow!" Ed had to admit it was pretty impressive. "But isn't it about time he got a proper job – at his age?"

"Skateboarding *is* a proper job, Dad. He's a multimillionaire!" Sam looked at him with wide eyes. "That's what I'm going to do when I grow up."

"How many skateboard millionaires are there?"

"Loads!"

"Mmm."

"Dad, Pendruggan looks too lame to have a board park, but I saw some dudes with boards when we were driving back from that fish-and-chip shop. Can we go and find it? Please, Dad?"

"Maybe later. You hungry?"

"Do bears shit in the woods?"

"Sam, mind your language, mate."

"Sorry."

"The full works?"

"Yes!" Sam and his dad fist-bumped and Ed headed over to the open-plan kitchen. He hoped that Charlotte had picked up some supplies yesterday, though he hadn't noticed what was in the large selection of bags and holdalls when he'd unpacked her ancient Volvo. He opened the fridge door – it was a huge American-style one – and was pleased to see breakfast ingredients: eggs, bacon, sausages, mushrooms, plus a few peppers and onions, some milk, cheese and a loaf of bread. There was even fresh coffee in the cupboard. He smiled, relieved that he wouldn't have to tramp into the village before his caffeine fix.

He set about clattering around the kitchen, pulling out sauce- pans, frying pans and chopping boards. Breakfast was well on the way by the time Alex came downstairs. Her hair was scraped back in her trademark ponytail and she was rubbing sleep from her eyes.

"God, Dad, are you trying to wake the dead?"

"Good morning, my treasure!" He kissed her on the top of her head. "I like your jimjams." He pointed with his wooden spoon at her Hello Kitty pyjamas.

She threw him a sarcastic look. "They're ironic."

"Of course they are, my little princess."

Alex playfully gave him a push and then sat down next to her brother.

"Oh, no, not Spike Turner again."

"Feck off."

"Sam, enough with the potty mouth," Ed warned.

"*Feck* isn't a swearword, Dad."

"Don't push your luck."

The first proper bicker of the day was nipped in the bud by Molly's arrival as she bounded joyfully through the front door followed by Charlotte.

"It's a glorious day out there. Oh, good – breakfast. What are we having?"

"Don't interfere – you know this is my speciality."

"I wouldn't dream of it." She leaned in and gave Ed a peck on the cheek. "Though you do seem to have used every single pot, pan and utensil in the entire kitchen."

"It's a man thing. We need our man tools."

"It's an organisation thing – or lack of it – if you ask me."

"I didn't. Sam, Alex, I'm dishing up. Can you lay the table?"

There was then a chaotic scrum as the small kitchen was filled with three bodies all rummaging around in drawers and cupboards that they weren't familiar with, while Charlotte sat down at the table with the paper.

"That village shop's quite something. There's a funny woman in there, some ancient Cockney."

"Ah, that's Queenie, what she doesn't know isn't worth knowing. Right – here it comes." He set loaded plates in front of Charlotte and Sam, who fell on them eagerly. Then he went back for a pile of buttered toast. "Yours is coming, don't worry," he told Alex.

A moment later he was back with a plate for himself and one for his daughter. He was halfway through a Waitrose Cumberland sausage when he realised that Alex was still staring at her untouched plate.

"What's wrong?" he asked.

Charlotte looked up from her paper. "Oh."

"Oh, what?"

Everyone was looking from their plate to Ed. "What?"

"Dad, Alex is a vegetarian," Sam said through a mouthful of scrambled eggs.

"Since when?" Ed was flabbergasted. "The last time we ate out, you had that giant burger, remember? With two burgers, bacon and blue cheese – it was fifteen quid," he added, still aghast at the bill. Alex pursed her lips and put her head to one side, speaking to him in a patronising voice: "I've been meat-free for over a year now, Dad."

"Yes, that was probably the last time we went out for a meal," Charlotte said matter-of-factly. "And I can't remember the last time you sat down to a meal at home without jumping up to take a phone call or check your email every five minutes. You probably didn't notice."

"But you used to love my fry-ups." Ed was aware that a whine had entered his voice.

"I still do, Dad, but not with any of this." And she used her fork to push one of the sausages towards her father.

Ed was struck speechless. How had he managed to miss some- thing so obvious?

Charlotte reached out for her daughter's plate. "Want me to make you something else, darling?"

Determined to retrieve the situation, Ed leapt from his chair. "Hang on – give me a chance – what do you want instead? Poached eggs on toast? Welsh rarebit – have we got any cheese?"

"An omelette – a nice one and not too runny."

"Right," said Ed. "The perfect omelette on its way."

"Can I have Alex's bacon and sausage, then?" Sam was already moving his fork towards Alex's abandoned plate.

Charlotte laughed. "Here – go nuts. I'll put your dad's breakfast in the oven to keep warm."

A few minutes of banging and clattering ensued as Ed cleaned the frying pan and prepared the ingredients. The delicious smell of sautéed mushrooms and onions wafted over, until eventually Ed presented his daughter with a golden omelette, butter still bubbling away on the surface. "Well?" he asked anxiously. "Is it perfect?"

Alex put a forkful into her mouth and gave it a delicate chew. "Pretty much."

Ed breathed out. "That'll do."

Charlotte waved for him to sit down, then retrieved his half-full plate from the warm oven before rolling her sleeves up to tackle the huge pile of washing-up.

When he'd finished eating, Ed joined his wife at the sink, whispering, "So did I pull victory from the jaws of defeat?"

"Just about," she answered, not looking up from her task. "This time. But there's no such thing as perfection. Not in families and not in omelettes, either.

It takes practice to even be half good, let alone perfect."

"What do you mean?" Ed could tell there was a subtext to what she was saying, but he couldn't get a handle on it.

"I mean..." She put down the pan she was scouring and looked up at him. "You might be able to manufacture perfection on a three-day holiday, but it's much harder for me to do it every day at home in Worthing. On my own." She turned away to dry her hands on a tea towel, then tossed him a scouring pad. "Seeing as you're demonstrating how to be the perfect husband and father this weekend, how about doing the rest of the washing-up?"

Deciding that the best policy was to say nothing, Ed took the scouring pad and finished washing the dishes.

After breakfast, keen to make the most of the late-summer sunshine, they set off for the beach cabin. As they made their way down the path, they could see that, while the beach wasn't as busy as some of the sandy beaches in the area, Shellsand Bay had its own unique charm. With no direct road leading to the beach, it could be reached only from the path, which made access difficult for buggies and wheelchairs, and limited the number of casual visitors. But the Atlantic swell guaranteed excellent waves, making it a surfer's paradise, and it also had a devoted following among those who appreciated its natural beauty and sheltered position in the lee of the cliffs.

Charlotte had packed everything they needed for the day into their cooler bag and an assortment of beach bags. Although the sun was shining, there was a chill in the air, so she hadn't taken any chances, bringing along blankets, towels and cardigans in case the weather took a turn for the worse.

Once in the cabin, Ed pulled out the deckchairs and the wind- breaker, fashioning a little area in front of the veranda. The clap- board doors of the other beach huts were all padlocked, so they had that part of the beach to themselves.

Charlotte stuck the kettle on, pulling out some green teabags from one of the carriers. "Fancy a brew?" she asked Ed.

"Got any coffee?"

"There might be some in the dresser." She had a rummage in the cupboard and found a jar of Mellow Bird's. It was lumpy, but it would do.

Sam made straight for the surfboard and wetsuits.

"Come on, Dad – let's have a go."

Ed was reluctant but aware that he'd dragged them all down there and this might be the price he'd have to pay. Tall, at six foot four inches, he'd always felt like he was all clumsy legs, especially when dancing or roller-skating. Now in his forties, he was rarely required to do either, though he suspected that surfing might expose the same sort of awkward gangliness and lack of coordination.

"OK, why not? How do you get one of these things on?" he said with more enthusiasm than he felt.

While Ed and Sam pulled out the squeaky rubbery suits and tried to work out which part went where, Alex plonked herself down on one of the deckchairs and pulled a book from her bag.

Charlotte, meanwhile, was busy exploring. Next to the cupboard was a little, bleached, white wooden table about waist height. There was a gingham curtain around it, and when she pulled it aside she could see a bowl and some washing-up liquid, as well as some tea towels. She'd noticed a standpipe on the beach at the bottom of the path, so that must be where the water came from. Cute. In fact, there were cute things all over the place, from frames filled with old seaside postcards and seaside knick-knacks adorning every surface.

"Now, where are the mugs?" she said to herself.

Opening the bottom of the dresser, she couldn't see any mugs but she did see something else which caught her eye. There were some very old board games, including snakes & ladders and ludo, Scrabble and Yahtzee, as well as a few jigsaw puzzles, but she also spied an old Tea Time biscuit tin. She pulled it out and prised the lid off. It was filled with colour pencils and a few sticks of charcoal. Peering further inside the cupboard, she could also see a supply of artist's paper and a couple of sketchpads. She pulled them out and flicked through the pages;

someone had already drawn several pretty pictures of the local area. One of them was of the cabin. It was a little amateur, but the colours and the flag were pretty accurate. Across the top of the picture the artist had written, 'The perfect place to be yourself '.

She smiled and gathered up all the materials – it would be the ideal beach occupation. And who knows? she thought. Maybe she would find herself again.

Hearing the sound of her husband's laughter, Charlotte looked up from her sketchpad. Despite Ed's protestations, Charlotte could see that he had quite taken to the surfboard. While their thrashing and floundering might not, strictly speaking, be classed as surfing, he and Sam seemed to be having a lot of fun.

In her own quiet way, she too was having fun. For the last couple of hours, she'd been trying to capture the scene in front of her. Drawing by the sea had been a favourite pastime of her childhood, back in the days when her parents would set up the windbreakers and sun shade and picnic hamper for long summer days on the beach near Weymouth. It was there that she'd acquired a lifelong fascination for the ever-changing colours of the sea and sky. No sooner had you picked out the subtle teal and turquoise tints of the waves than the clouds would shift and the tones would shift to purple and grey. After a couple of attempts she had decided it was impossible to capture a moment in time; better to be more impressionistic. The figures of Ed and Sam were fluid dashes, as was Molly, the rest of the holidaymakers and surfers mere traces against the cerulean blue of the sky and the cobalt brilliance of the sea.

She put down her pencil and scrutinised her work. Overall, she was pleased with it. She hadn't quite got the shade of the sky right, but she hadn't been aiming for perfection. Her stomach rumbled. Breakfast seemed hours ago.

As if on cue, dripping with sea spray, her son and husband came running towards her.

"Mum, the sea's freezing! Even with the suits on, it's wicked. What's for lunch?"

"You're a bottomless pit, Sam Appleby." Though only eleven, Sam was already shooting up and looked set to be as tall as his father. "Sausage sandwiches for you. Cheese for Alex. Egg-mayo for anybody."

Sam narrowed his eyes. "Normal egg-mayo?"

"Yes. Normal egg-mayo."

"You didn't put anything weird in it – not like last time?"

Charlotte feigned shock. "I don't know what you could possibly mean. Of course there's nothing 'weird' in the egg-mayonnaise sandwiches. What a funny boy you are!"

Sam wasn't convinced. "I'll have sausage. What've you been doing, Mum?"

"Mum's been working on that drawing for ages," Alex said, putting down her book and springing to her feet. "Come on, show us."

Alex and Sam peered over her shoulder at the sketch, Sam dripping seawater on the page.

"Careful."

"Wow, Mum, that's reeeeally good!" Sam congratulated her.

Charlotte couldn't help preening slightly.

"Well, *I* quite like it."

Alex feigned indifference. "Yeah, it's OK. I forgot that you used to be an artist or something."

"What do you mean, 'used to be'?" Charlotte bristled.

"I mean before, when you had a proper job. Wasn't it something to do with art?"

Charlotte instantly made the transition from bristling to prickly. "For your information, I was a design director on a number of TV programmes and films. Yes, it was something to do with art and, yes, you do need to be quite good at it. As far as I know you don't stop being artistic just because your womb has been commandeered for the purpose of having children. The two aren't mutually exclusive, you know!"

Alex merely shrugged and looked bored, returning to her deck- chair and her book.

Charlotte stood, hands on hips, glaring.

"Look, love, I don't think Alex meant anything," said Ed, trying to smooth her ruffled feathers. "She wasn't thinking, that's all."

Still fuming, Charlotte turned her glare on Ed, who attempted what he hoped was a concerned and sympathetic smile. To her it seemed condescending.

"It's an incredible picture," he gushed, digging himself in deeper. "And I think it's great that you've found an outlet for your creativity while we're here."

For a split second, Charlotte felt like strangling him. Instead, she said through gritted teeth, "Could you try and be a little more patronising, Ed. You're almost there, but you've not quite managed to make me feel completely, utterly belittled – though you're obviously trying very hard."

Ed's face fell. Charlotte felt a twinge of guilt for turning on him, but it was too late. Her anger was in full flow.

"How do you know that I don't already have an outlet for my creativity, Ed?" she went on, her voice rising an octave or two. "Though it would actually be quite difficult, wouldn't it, seeing as I'm raising our children practically on my own? I'm not surprised they've forgotten what I'm capable of – all they ever see is the mum who cooks, cleans and nags!"

"Charlotte, I'm sorry, I didn't mean—"

"Oh, forget it. I'm going to take Molly for a walk and stretch my legs."

She grabbed Molly's lead from the rail and Molly shot out from the beach cabin where she'd been keeping out of the sun. "Come on, Mol, let's go!" she called, striding off in the direction of the cliff path without so much as a backward glance as she added, "The sandwiches are in the cooler box. Help yourself."

🐚

Ed took a bite of egg-mayonnaise sandwich. As the first tang hit his taste buds, he realised that there was something mixed in with the egg and the mayonnaise, something that crunched and that didn't quite work. It tasted odd. He put it back in the sandwich bag.

"Where's Mum gone?" Alex plonked herself down next to him.

"For a walk."

"Is she in a huff?"

"Possibly."

"Sorry." Alex drew a circle in the sand and looked sheepish.

"Never mind. As much my fault as yours, and you know it won't last."

"Why isn't Mum a… design director any more?"

Ed sighed and wondered how to put it. "Working in film and TV isn't exactly compatible with a normal family life. The hours are crap and production companies don't tend to make allowances for working mothers. The two don't mix."

"She likes her job at the theatre."

"How do you know?"

"She's always on the phone to Henry talking about it. He's the director. She spends most of her time at the theatre. Sometimes she asks me to be at home for Sam when he gets back from school because she's running late."

Ed felt a hot flush rush up his face and tried not to focus on what could be making her late. *I love you… can't live without you…*

"Will Mum ever go back to work properly? Like before?"

He started to answer but then realised he had no idea whether Charlotte had ambitions in that direction. When the children were little, Charlotte hadn't wanted to leave them, but once they were both at school they had discussed the possibilities. Ed knew that Charlotte missed her work. But jobs were few and far between, and those that did come were either too far away or the hours couldn't fit around the children. Eventually, the subject was quietly dropped. Ed's career had taken off and Charlotte had seemed content to help out at the local theatre, which put on short runs that were geared towards families. "I don't know, Alex," he sighed.

"Dad, there's someone waving at you – over there."

"Where?"

Alex pointed at a woman coming down the path. "Put your glasses on, Dad!"

Ed scrabbled around in the sand for his specs and put them on. The blur formed itself into Penny coming into view. He smiled widely and waved her over.

"Good God – Alexandra, is that you?" Penny exclaimed when she saw Alex. "You're just like your father!"

"Hopefully she'll grow out of it. Hello, Pen." Ed stood and gave her a big hug.

"Hi, Penny." Alex gave Penny a hug too before joining her brother and Penny waved to Sam who waved his spade back in return.

"How's it going?" she asked. "This is an amazing place, isn't it? It has a completely different feel when you're not working."

"I know. It's perfect. Well... almost."

"Where's Charlotte?"

"Um, she's gone for a walk."

"Things still a bit rocky?"

"Maybe."

"Give her time – *your* time. And don't give up."

He ran his hands through his hair. "I'm trying."

"Isn't that Charlotte coming down the path?"

Ed turned and saw his wife heading towards them with Molly. The tense bad humour was gone from her face, but there was a definite flicker of caution in her eyes when she registered Penny Leighton's presence – effectively her husband's boss.

"Hi, Pen, lovely to see you!" Charlotte gave Penny a hug. They knew each other well.

"Have you been walking on the cliffs? Majestic, aren't they?"

"Yes, and the perfect antidote to disappearing up my own arse." Charlotte shot Ed a quick glance. "Not trying to drag my husband away from his holiday, are you, Pen?" She said this lightly, but Ed knew there'd be trouble if he reneged on his promise.

"Not on your nelly! Simon's banned me from talking about work, so no worries on that score."

"How's your lovely daughter, Jenna?"

"Exhausting! But we've got a night off this evening. Why don't you all come and

127

join us for dinner at the Dolphin later?
Don and Dorrie are doing a hog roast and
all the locals will be there."

Charlotte looked at Ed, uncertain.

"No work talk, we promise – don't
we, Pen?"

"Brownie's honour."

It took Charlotte a nanosecond to
make up her mind. "You're on!" She gave
Penny a huge grin. "I could do with a pint
of Cornish Knocker!"

The Dolphin was packed out.
Holidaymakers and locals alike seemed
to be making the most of summer's last
hurrah. Ed, Charlotte and the kids made

their way through the throng and found that Penny and her husband, Simon, the local vicar had saved them a seat at a table with two of their friends: Helen Merrifield and Piran Ambrose.

They all shook hands and said their hellos, then Piran, Simon and Ed duly trooped to the bar, as men do, while the women got chatting about life and kids.

Charlotte warmed to Helen immediately. It came as a surprise that Helen was now a grandmother – Charlotte thought she was way too young. And she seemed so at home in the community that it was hard to believe she'd left her husband and moved down here from London only recently.

"I thought Piran was your husband."

"Good God, no!" Helen laughed. "We'd end up killing each other. I've been there, done that, and he's way too grouchy to be a full-time boyfriend. I know you've got to take the rough with the smooth, but he takes the biscuit sometimes, so it's better this way."

It turned out that Helen lived a few doors down from their holiday let, in Gull's Cry – the cottage she'd admired when she arrived.

Helen clapped her hands. "Fabulous, I can take you for a tour round the village. I'll introduce you to Queenie and Tony."

"Oh, yes, I've already met Queenie."

The men rejoined them at the table. "Guess what: Piran's a proper Cornish fisherman!" announced Ed. He had a boyish flush, and Charlotte suspected he was already a bit pissed, but she was glad to see that he was enjoying himself.

Piran gave them a stern look. "Proper fisherman are the only kind we have in this part of the world. 'Tis a serious business."

"Yes, of course. I'm not much of a fisherman myself. I only went once with my dad, and neither of us could bear to kill the poor buggers. We threw most of them back in."

"I could never, ever kill a fish. They have the same feelings as people and catching them is murder!" Alex said with feeling, looking up from her iPad.

A smile danced around Piran's lips. "Aye, maid, their lives is as precious to them as yours is to you. All good fisherman respect that and only take what they need."

"Ha, that's funny, Alex," continued Ed, getting into his stride. "I seem to remember that you ended up killing quite a lot of fish when you were younger. Your fish tank had what you might call a revolving-door policy!"

"That wasn't the same thing, Dad!" she protested, but she laughed along with everyone else.

"At least it can't be as bad as Mum," Sam chipped in. "She's been prosecuted for crimes against fish dinners! Harry Potter wants her prawn surprise recipe so he can use it to defeat Voldemort!"

"You don't appreciate fine dining, that's your problem," protested Charlotte, but she was laughing too.

The laughter was interrupted by Alex's ringtone, which was an incredibly loud and annoying jangle.

She looked at the caller and answered it quickly, whispering into the phone that she'd call back when she was alone.

"Got a secret admirer, Alex?" Ed joked. "Make sure you don't bring him home on prawn-surprise night – that might be the last we see of him!"

Alex's face went puce and she balled her fists.

"Ed, hang on..." Charlotte could see immediately that Alex was upset. But Alex had already stood up and was facing her father, blushing hotly.

"You don't know what you're talking about. You don't understand and you don't even care!" Then she stomped off to sit outside on the terrace.

"What did I say?" Ed looked aghast, stung by the ferocity of her words.

"Teenagers – they're a mystery," said Simon, with a sympathetic shake of his head.

"It's getting late. Perhaps we should go." Charlotte started gathering up their things, casting anxious glances out to the terrace, where Alex could be seen furiously texting on her phone.

They all said their goodnights, Helen and Charlotte promising to see each other again. Charlotte retrieved Alex from the beer garden and the two of them walked on ahead with Sam and Molly, while Ed followed gloomily behind.

"She seemed so angry," he said to Charlotte hours later as they lay in bed. Outside the night air was still, punctuated occasionally by a barn owl emitting its blood-curdling scream as it swooped on its prey. "I've never seen her like that before."

"She's very touchy." Charlotte said sleepily from her side of the bed.

"But it's so unlike Alex. She hates confrontation, even if she *is* a sulky teenager."

Charlotte sighed from the depths of her pillow, then propped herself up on her elbows and turned to face Ed. "She's been like this for a while now. Something's bothering her, but she won't confide in me. If you'd been around more, you might have noticed before now."

There was no vitriol or accusation in her words – it was a merely bald statement. They both knew the truth of it and there was nothing Ed could say in his defence.

He ran a hand over his face. "I know, I know – it's just been so hard to get home. Maybe I can reschedule a few things, put a few projects on the back burner…"

"Ed." Charlotte lifted her hand to still his words. "This isn't about 'rescheduling a few things'. Alex is growing up. In a few years she'll be an adult. That's something no one can reschedule. And, if you don't adjust your priorities, you're going to miss what's left of her childhood. Sam's, too. Before you know it, they'll have drifted away from you and you'll never be able to get back what you've lost." Her voice softened as she saw the impact her words were having. "Right now, Alex needs us – even if she doesn't realise it." Then Charlotte turned her back on him and settled herself down to sleep. As her breathing deepened and she drifted off, Ed noticed a tightness grip his jaw and recognised the familiar feel of a long sleepless night ahead of him.

4

Typically for an English summer, a day of sunshine and blue skies was followed by a gloomy, overcast morning with ominous grey clouds threatening rain. The weather seemed to affect the mood in the cottage and, despite Ed's entreaties, Alex was refusing his offer of a vegetarian fry-up.

"I only want toast, Dad."

Alex was huddled up beneath the duvet in her bedroom, wrapped in her hoodie. Ed thought she looked much younger than her fifteen years.

"Come on, kitten," he coaxed. "A bite to eat and then we can take a trip somewhere. There's a lot to see around here. How about driving to Tintagel? There's a castle."

"I don't want to tramp round a boring castle."

"It's not boring – they say King Arthur was born there."

"Who?"

There'd been a time when Ed could shake his daughter out of a moody spell in minutes. Alex had been a naturally sunny child who was easily reduced to helpless giggles. He realised with a pang of disappointment that those days were gone. Getting a laugh today would be like getting blood out of a stone.

"Brown or white?"

"Brown. White bread is full of additives."

"So virtuous – aren't you supposed to be living on McDonald's and alcopops at your age?"

Ed's attempt at playful banter merely drew a roll of the eyes before Alex pulled the duvet over her head, signalling an end to the conversation. Defeated, he headed back downstairs.

Charlotte was putting on her waterproof and Sam was in his usual spot on the sofa, watching an episode of *The Big Bang Theory*.

"Off somewhere?" he asked his wife.

"I'm going to take a walk down to the beach hut with Molly."

"But it looks like rain. I was going to make breakfast."

"Not for me."

"Oh. What about you, Sam? Not going to reject the only meal I'm any good at, are you?"

"Nah, I'm starving. Is it ready now?"

Ed looked in the fridge. Their supplies had been somewhat depleted since yesterday. "We'll need to go on a foraging expedition. We're running low."

"Try that shop I was telling you about in the village," suggested Charlotte.

"Huh?"

"Ed, you'll have me doubting that you hang on my every word if you say things like that. I nipped in there for a paper yesterday morning – you can't miss it: the windows are lined with yellow cellophane and crammed with old boxes of Black Magic and York Fruits. It's as if the last fifty years never happened. The owner's an old Cockney—"

"Oh, you mean Queenie's shop. She does lovely pasties – or 'oggys' as they call them round here. You have to order them in advance though. The crew practically live off them when we're filming."

"Well, I think you'll find she sells groceries and everything else we need to top up our dwindling supplies. I can't believe you've been coming here year after year and you don't even know where to buy a loaf and a pint of milk."

"OK, Queenie's it is, then. Fancy a trip out, Sam?"

"Aw, I'm watching this!"

"You can watch that any time. Queenie's has to be seen to believed."

Leaving Ed to take on the parental duty of tearing his son away from the TV, Charlotte clipped Molly's lead onto her collar and opened the door. It was starting to rain, but she didn't care. The beach cabin was calling her.

By the time Charlotte got down the path to the beach, a steady drizzle had set in. Nothing too heavy, but enough to keep most people away. Aside from the odd dog-walker passing by, she had the beach all to herself.

She had left some dog towels in the cabin the day before and the first thing she did after undoing the padlock was to fish them out and give Molly a good rubdown. Molly looked out from behind the long hair that covered her eyes and groaned.

"Don't moan – I get enough of that from the kids! I know you hate the rain, but everything will end up smelling of wet dog if I don't dry you off."

Molly licked her face by way of apology and, once that was done, she settled down on her dog blanket while Charlotte put the kettle on.

Looking out at the turbulent greys and greens of the surf, whipped up by the rain, Charlotte thought she liked the beach even more today. There was something wonderfully liberating about being here alone. She'd had to get used to being by herself, with Ed away from home so much, but this was a different type of alone. Solitude rather than loneliness. She liked it. The thought of having this on your doorstep every day was hugely appealing and she could see why Helen had come to Pendruggan and stayed put. Maybe when the kids were older...

She dismissed the thought. No good daydreaming about something that could never happen – not the way things were.

Taking her sketchpad and pencils from the cupboard, she settled herself down on a deckchair on the veranda, well out of the rain. Then she began to draw.

Charlotte had completely lost track of time when a voice broke her concentration. On looking up she was surprised and delighted to see Helen Merrifield, accompanied by a lively Jack Russell terrier who danced around her feet. Helen hailed her and headed over. Charlotte waved back, laid her drawing down by the deckchair and put the kettle on. She had no idea how long she'd been there but the weather had brightened.

"Good afternoon, Charlotte. How are you today?"

"Afternoon? What time is it?"

Helen looked at her watch. "Coming up to one o'clock."

"Crikey! I've been here for hours. Cuppa?"

"Yes, please, I'm parched."

Helen pulled out another deckchair and plonked herself down on it, watching as her Jack Russell greeted Molly, the pair of them nose to nose, tails wagging, and then sniffing each other's bum in a doggy hello.

"What's your dog's name?" asked Charlotte.

"Jack – and he's not mine, he belongs Piran, in as much as he belongs to anyone. He's a law unto himself, that dog. He seems to have taken a fancy to yours."

Jack was chasing Molly in circles around the beach. Despite the difference in size, Jack seemed to have the upper hand.

Charlotte laughed. "Poor Molly, she's like a giddy schoolgirl. Has Jack been neutered?"

Helen snorted. "No dog of Piran's would have his knackers tampered with. Molly?"

"No idea. Don't think so..."

"Oh, well, a marriage made in heaven. The mind boggles. Is that your drawing?" Helen picked up the sketchpad from her feet. The picture was a brooding mass of greys and greens, depicting the turbulent surf of earlier. The colours were vivid and dramatic and the picture perfectly caught the atmosphere of Shellsand Bay. "You're very good, Charlotte. Is this the sort of thing you do at the theatre you were telling me about?"

"Not quite." Charlotte joined her, handing over a mug of steaming English breakfast tea. It wasn't a green-tea sort of day. "The sets are bigger, so you can't be so precise. It's more about getting the right feel for a production and creating a canvas that helps the performers tell the story. You have to think a bit differently."

"Do you enjoy it?"

Charlotte thought for a moment, looking out to the horizon. "Yes, I do. It's not the same as working on TV sets, not as exhilarating, but you get to be creative. You have to work very closely with the director, channelling his vision..." she trailed off and Helen could sense something beneath.

"I can imagine. It's a collaboration."

"Yes, Henry's been very..." – Charlotte searched for the right word – "supportive."

Helen didn't pry further. "How's the holiday?"

"Oh, not too bad. The usual bickering, but it's always like that, isn't it?"

"Tell me about it!" Helen said with feeling. "I've lost count of the family holidays that have been marred by squabbles and mood swings and tantrums. They can be quite a trial. All too often it's a relief to go home."

Charlotte shook her head. "It's nowhere near as bad as that. It makes a nice change for us to be together. And this is absolutely wonderful." She threw her hand out expansively at Shellsand Bay. "It's just..."

"You don't need to tell me," Helen said sympathetically. "It's hard for everyone to rub along sometimes, isn't it? Families change and grow, and not always at the same rate. I had a husband who spent most of our holidays chatting up the barmaid or trying to cadge telephone numbers from young waitresses. One day I woke up and realised that, while I'd changed and matured, my silly husband Gray was still the same insecure man-child he'd been twenty-odd years ago. It was liberating to realise I wasn't going to put up with it any more."

Charlotte nodded. "Yes, we do change. I can't even remember what I was like when Ed and I first met. I must have been quite confident, but I think it was more bravado than anything. Ed was so intense, took everything so seriously." She watched a small boat chugging far out at sea, tossed gently by the waves. "He still does take it all so seriously. I know he seems like a lovely easygoing guy, but he's a worrier, forever driving himself, like he's on a treadmill he can't get off of."

Helen sipped at her tea. "Maybe you should swap roles for a while."

"He'd never be able to do that."

"Try him. You never know."

Charlotte frowned, thinking.

"Why not suggest that you both give it a trial run?" said Helen. "He should embrace change and so should you. If your marriage is solid, then it'll be good for both of you – sometimes a marriage needs a helping hand to get it over that midlife hump. None of us stay the same all our lives, we grow and we change – it's human nature."

"Maybe." Charlotte didn't look convinced. Was their marriage solid? "Are you going back up to the village now? I'll come with you."

They packed up and Charlotte put Molly on the lead. Jack didn't have one.

"Got time for that village tour? We can pop in and say hello to Polly, who lives next door to me."

"Why not?"

"By the way, Piran's offered to take you all out on his boat – the weather looks like it's going in the right direction, so how about this afternoon?"

"What a great idea! Thanks, Helen."

"It's no problem. I'll text Piran."

"Not just for that... I mean, you know... the tea and sympathy."

"Any time."

The two women exchanged a hug and headed back towards Pendruggan.

***

Charlotte loved Polly's cottage. It was full of wind chimes and the scent of jasmine. Polly gave her some Tregothan tea – "It's good for your chakras" – and she fed Molly an organic vegetarian dog treat, which Molly ate politely though with a certain lack of enthusiasm.

There was a bounce in Charlotte's step when she got back to the cottage to find

Ed and Sam on the sofa watching surf videos on YouTube.

"We went to Queenie's," Ed told her. "I'm afraid she didn't have any oggys left for our lunch, but I got some stuff for sandwiches."

"Mum, come and have a look at this," Sam said. "We've been watching these huge waves and—"

"Put that thing away. The sun's shining and we're going out for the afternoon."

She skipped up the stairs to find Alex still in her room. "Hey. How's it going?"

Alex grunted something incomprehensible from beneath her hoodie.

"Sun's out."

"I don't like the sun."

Charlotte laughed. "Or anything else for that matter, it seems. Stop hibernating, let's go out."

"I'm tired. I don't want to tramp round a stately home or a lobster farm."

"Ah – I've got something much better than that in mind."

Alex's interest was piqued. "Like what?"

"Fancy a trip out on a fishing boat?"

Alex sat up – she loved boats. "Piran's?"

"Who else's!"

"Awesome! When are we going?"

"Now?"

Alex jumped out of bed and Charlotte headed back downstairs to rally the troops.

An hour later they headed out of Trevay on Piran's fishing boat. The rain had cleared and the sun kept breaking through the clouds, promising warmer weather to come. The family foursome were all decked out in lifejackets and chatting excitedly as the boat chugged out into the open sea.

"Backalong times, Trevay was full of little boats and fishermen like me," Piran informed them. "Nowadays, it's the big boys like Behenna and Clovelly Fisheries what gets the big catches, but some of us still stick to the old ways."

They spent the next few hours learning about tackle and lines. Despite his gruff manner, Piran was a patient and thoughtful teacher. Alex and Ed were in their element. Alex had always been fascinated by how things work, and Piran's informed explanation of long-line fishing and how to set the lines near the surface kept her completely absorbed.

Sam and Charlotte were more interested in watching the wildlife. They thought they saw a dolphin's fin and definitely spotted a couple of seals popping their heads out of the water, eyeing them curiously.

"I've caught some!" Alex was thrilled when she felt the tug of mackerel on her line. Neither Ed nor Charlotte wanted to spoil the mood by reminding her of her vegetarian principles.

After a happy afternoon, they headed back towards Trevay. To everyone's delight, a pod of dolphins appeared alongside the boat and raced them for a few minutes before breaking off and disappearing back under the waves. Charlotte watched in awe as the lithe creatures darted beneath the water. She remembered that the ancient Celts believed that dolphins had healing powers. Was it too much to hope that this could be the start of the healing process for her family too?

When they pulled into the harbour and unloaded their catch, everyone agreed that a barbie down on the beach would be the perfect end to a perfect day. Charlotte filled a cooler box with ingredients that Ed had picked up from Queenie's shop, along with their fish.

Aside from a fry-up, Ed's other speciality was a barbecue. He loved the rigmarole of setting the charcoal – never briquettes – getting the glow just right, and then judging with minute precision whether it was time to put the food on. No charred-on-the-outside-raw-on-the-inside frozen sausages on *his* watch.

As Ed set the barbecue going in the fading evening sunlight, Sam tackled Alex about her mackerel, half a dozen of which hung from a string attached to a hook outside the cabin.

"If you're a vegetarian, how come you've gone fishing?"

Charlotte held her breath for a moment, fearing that the blue touchpaper had been lit and an explosion would surely follow.

But, after taking a moment to consider her response, Alex said calmly, "Fishing felt different than I thought it would. Piran explained that fishing didn't have to be destructive as long as you fish responsibly and think about your impact on the environment. I liked setting the lines and doing it properly."

"Are you going to eat one?"

"I'm not sure."

"Well, I'm hoping they'll be delicious," Ed chipped in. "But I wish we'd asked Piran to gut them as well."

"He'd have told you not to be a 'bleddy lazy up-country arse' and to do it yourself." Charlotte came alongside him, carrying a chopping board and a plastic bowl filled with new potatoes and some beetroot, which she placed on the camping table. "What are you going to cook them in?"

"I've got a marinade of lime, ginger and chilli."

"Nice! I'm starving." She handed him an open beer and took a swig from her own.

"Cheers." They chinked bottles.

As the cooking got under way, the appetising smell from the fish was unbearably tempting and Alex found herself hovering by her dad as he dished hot fish onto plates.

"Want some?" he offered non-judgementally.

"Go on then." She picked hot chunks of mackerel off with her fingers and declared them delicious.

"Does this mean you're not a vegetarian now?" Sam badgered.

"I'm a fishetarian!"

There were plenty of other people down at the beach that evening and they stayed on until quite late. Charlotte was disappointed to see that her potato, beetroot and egg salad remained untouched. She was sure that was the list of ingredients that Lorraine Pascale had used... But maybe the egg was wrong – or was it the beetroot? She offered it to Molly, who gave her a courteous thank-you lick but left the bowl untouched.

When they got home, Charlotte tidied away the things while Ed collapsed on the sofa and the children drifted off upstairs to bed.

Charlotte poured herself a glass of red wine and one for Ed, but by the time she sat down, squeezed onto the sofa in the tiny space left by his big long legs, he was fast asleep and snoring loudly.

Noticing that his glasses had fallen halfway off his face, she removed them. He never carried a spare pair and would be lost if they got broken. Looking at him now, she thought that, apart from the grey hair around his temples, he looked almost exactly the same as he had when they'd first met. Essentially, he was the same, she realised. Constant. Steady. Just never there these days... She wondered what he would say about her.

Charlotte took a blanket and gently tucked it around him, then turned and headed to bed with Molly close behind her.

5

It was the Applebys' last day in
Pendruggan. Tomorrow Charlotte and
the kids would be going home, and
Charlotte was surprised how sad she felt
at the idea. She'd fallen in love with the
place. As she looked around her at the
dozens of families, surfers and walkers
who had come to Shellsand Beach to
enjoy the late-August sunshine, she
thought there was no better place to be
than here.

Their imminent departure meant the time for prevaricating was over. Charlotte would have to talk to Ed today. She'd decided what she was going to say and how she was going to say it – she'd have to pick her moment.

For the first time since they'd been on Shellsand Bay, there was a sign of life from one of the other cabins. The one next door to theirs was occupied. It looked to Charlotte like a family of surfers. There was an older man – a well-preserved specimen, perhaps in his late forties – accompanied by a young man who looked to be just out of his teens, and another lad about the same age as Alex. The younger two had blond hair, while the older one had probably been blond once but his hair was now white, with thick Boris Becker eyebrows that stood out in stark contrast against his tanned skin. All three had the sort of tan that comes from year-round exposure to the Cornish elements rather than a few weeks on the beach in summer.

The man was immediately friendly and introduced himself in a thick Cornish burr as Paul Tallack. "We'm from up Trevay way, but my boys love the waves. Older one's Ryan and my youngest is Josh over there."

He and Ed shook hands. "This is Charlotte, my wife, and those are my kids, Alex and Sam." He pointed to his son and daughter, down at the water's edge. "You're surfing too?"

"Aye, love it. We all do. Shellsand's got the right climate, see? Today's going be perfect. Them waves is building."

"How can you tell?"

Paul tapped his nose conspiratorially, then laughed. "You gotta be in the know. Seriously, I'm a reserve coastguard, so I've spent years watching the waves and learning. You can never second-guess the sea, though. That's part of the wonder of it. Never know what you're gonna get. Need to respect it too, mind – can't take any chances."

Spotting the presence of real-life surfers, Sam came hurrying up the beach to watch Ryan expertly setting out their kit. Charlotte could see that her husband and son were bonding with the neighbours in that way men do. Perhaps Sam and Ed were going to get that surfing lesson they so desperately needed after all.

Josh, the younger of the two sons, ambled over to where Alex was sitting, still with her head in a book, trying hard to be noncha- lant. At about fifteen or sixteen he was already a handsome young man and had that characteristic and confident Cornish charm.

"What you'm reading?"

"Pardon?" Charlotte looked up from her book. "Your book. What is it?"

"Umm," Alex looked down awkwardly at the cover, as if she'd forgotten. "It's called *The Catcher in the Rye*." She looked down at her book again, her cheeks suddenly bright pink.

Watching from the veranda, Charlotte felt a pang at Alex's awkwardness, but Josh didn't seem to notice. "What's it about?" He sat down next to her as if it was the most natural thing in the world.

Alex hesitated, looking around her as if to find somewhere to bolt to. But there was no escape. She caught her mother's eye and Charlotte looked away quickly, desperate not to add to her daughter's shyness.

"Er, it's about a boy – he doesn't feel that the world understands him. Or that he doesn't understand the world. He sort of goes off on his own..." She trailed off awkwardly.

"Yeah, folks are like that. My dad's all right, leaves me alone, but my mum's always on at us: 'Do this, don't do that, pick your trainers up.' She don't stop..."

Josh continued in this lively vein and Charlotte smiled. Alex didn't stand a chance.

The sun was high in the sky. Paul and Ryan couldn't have been happier to share their expertise, and in Ed and Sam they had two ultra-willing pupils. Josh seemed content to forgo surfing and sit with Alex. The two of them were now side by side on the deckchairs, chatting animatedly. Alex's face was lit up in a way Charlotte had almost forgotten, it was so long since she'd seen her that happy. Josh obviously had the knack of breaking down her barriers – his charm offensive was working wonders where Charlotte's and Ed's had failed. Maybe she'd been worrying too much.

When lunchtime arrived, Paul and Ed decided to pool resources on the barbecue front. Was it possible for two men to share barbecue duties? Charlotte wondered. Or would it end in a tongs-off? They seemed to be doing all right, though she almost wished they weren't. Having steeled herself for a difficult conversation with Ed, she was anxious to get it over with. But first they needed a moment alone. A little voice kept niggling away at her: *If you don't tell him now...* Her thoughts were interrupted by Paul's voice booming across the beach: "C'mon, Josh – muck in, mate! Get back to the jeep and bring me some more o' that charcoal, it's in the boot."

Josh did as he was asked and Alex came over to sit with her mother on the veranda.

"You've caught the sun." Charlotte observed. "Given up on the vampire look, then?"

"Mum!" But Alex was smiling.

They were joined by Sam, who proceeded to strip off his wetsuit, scattering big drops of seawater over both of them.

"Watch out, you flippin' idiot!" Alex scolded.

"Don't call me an idiot. At least I'm not sitting there with an idiotic look on my face mooning over some stupid boy."

"Shuttup, you little arsehole!"

"Sam," said Charlotte sharply, "stop showing off. Alex, calm down and don't let him wind you up."

But Sam was in that irksome mode that comes as second nature to eleven-year-old boys, and, having discovered Alex's raw spot, he wasn't about to stop poking it.

"Oohhh, feeling sensitive about your new boyfriend?" He puckered up his lips and made loud kissing noises. "Mwah-mwah, I love you, Joshy."

"I'm going to kill you if you don't shut up, you little shit!"

"Sam, that's enough!" Charlotte could see that Sam was pushing it too far, but there was no letup.

"Alex and Joshy, sitting in a tree," he sang, "K-I-S-S-I-N-G!"

At this Alex launched herself at Sam, shoving him to the ground and kicking him in the ribs, screaming. "I hate you! I wish you were dead! I hate you and I hate Josh – I hate all boys!"

Despite thinking that Sam had gone too far, Charlotte was shocked at Alex's reaction.

Ed, hearing the fracas, rushed over and hauled the children apart. "What the hell's going on, you two?"

"That cow pushed me over and kicked me!"

Sam was rubbing his ribs and feigning tears, but Alex was panting hard and real tears of anger were streaming down her face.

Ed took her by the shoulders. "Alex, relax. Come on, let's chill for a minute, OK?"

"No, it's not OK." Alex shook her head violently. "Don't tell me to chill out. Leave me alone." She shrugged her father off and moved away.

"Alex, please, talk to me—"

"No. Leave me alone, all of you. I'm going to take Molly for walk." And, before he could stop her, Alex grabbed Molly, who'd been tethered to the veranda to stop her going near the barbecue, and stormed off in the direction of the path.

"Ed? I'm not sure we should let her go off like this..."

"Let's give her some space, Charlotte."

"I don't know – she seems really upset."

"She just needs a bit of time to calm down, that's all. As for you..." Ed turned to Sam and launched into a serious telling off. Charlotte caught snatches of it drifting on the breeze – *no iPad* and *apologise to your sister* – but her thoughts were with Alex as she watched her climb the path up the cliffs.

🐚

Over forty minutes had gone by and Alex still hadn't returned. The food had been dished up but neither Charlotte nor Ed could muster an appetite. Even Josh was asking after her now.

"I'm going to go and look for her," announced Charlotte.

"No, I'll go."

Their conversation was interrupted as the insistent beep of a pager came from Paul's pocket. He took it out, looked at it and then made a call on his mobile.

"OK, mate. I'm on my way." He rang off. Gone was his carefree, happy-go-lucky demeanour. He turned back to them with a look of tense concern. "There's no need to panic yet, but a fishing boat on the water close to here has reported a sighting of a body down on the rocks."

Charlotte's hand flew to her mouth. "Oh, my God! Alex!"

"Now hang on a minute," said Paul, laying a reassuring hand on her arm. "There's no reason to assume that it's Alex. The best thing you can do is stay here in case she comes back. I'm on callout and we've been scrambled. We'll let you know if there's any news."

As Paul set off at a run up the cliff path in the direction of his jeep, Charlotte and Ed looked at each other. "I'm going to find her, Ed.' Charlotte's tone brooked no argument.

"I'm coming with you." Ed was equally determined. Sam's bottom lip trembled and Ed squeezed his son's shoulder. "Stay with Ryan and Josh, Sam. Everything's going to be OK, I promise."

Keen ramblers could walk all the way from Pendruggan to Trevay, but Charlotte had never been that far. On her walks with Molly they had only pottered along a short section where slopes dotted with gorse and heather rolled gently down to the sea. Now she found herself on a stretch of the coast path with brambles on one side and vertiginous cliffs on the other. She could hardly bear to look down to where the waves battered the rocks a couple of hundred feet below.

"I'll never forgive myself if anything's happened to her..." Charlotte's voice caught as she hurried along the path with Ed on her heels. "I should never have let her go – I could see how upset she was."

"Try not to think the worst. We don't know that anything's happened – she might be back at the cottage, playing with her iPad." But Ed wasn't sure that he believed his own words. Alex might be fifteen, but she wasn't worldly wise and she'd been upset and angry – the possibilities didn't bear thinking about.

They'd been walking for twenty minutes now and there was still no sign of her. Ed had tried calling her mobile, but there was no signal. Charlotte could feel panic rising up inside her with each step. Striding out in front, she picked up her pace. *Please, please, let her be all right,* she prayed.

Then she saw a familiar outline ahead. Alex!

"Darling! Alex! We're here!" Charlotte ran as fast as she dared to where Alex was crouched down, almost at the edge of the cliff. On hearing her mother's voice, Alex stood and threw herself at her mother. The pair of them were immediately enveloped by Ed's strong arms, and for a moment they stood hugging each other and crying.

"M-m-m—"Alex was distraught, tears choking her words. Charlotte held her tightly, whispering soothing words. "It's all right, baby, it's all right, we're here."

"M-M-Molly—m Alex could only point down to the rocks below.

"You two, get back from the edge." Ed took a step forward and peered down the face of the cliff. The drop here wasn't so sharp and the cliff sloped down a little more gently, but down at the bottom of the rocks he could see the unmistakable hairy body of Molly. She didn't appear to be moving.

Despite a surge of relief that it was his dog and not his daughter lying down there, he felt a lump in his throat at the sight below. Behind him, Charlotte was asking, "Do you know how it happened, Alex?"

Between convulsive sobs, Alex replied, "We were walking… she wasn't on the lead and then she saw a rabbit… and then she was gone…"

"OK, baby, OK."

"I didn't want to leave her, Dad. I tried to call for help, but I couldn't get a signal… At first she was barking, and I was telling her it was going to be all right, but I couldn't see any way to get down to her… And now she's not moving." Alex broke into fresh tears.

"The main thing is to get you to safety. Charlotte, can you and Alex make it back to the beach? I'll wait here for the coastguard."

"OK." Charlotte gave her husband a brief but fierce hug and he kissed them both on their heads.

As they headed back up the path, Ed dropped to his knees and looked down at Molly's prone body.

"Hang on in there, girl," he whispered as the outline of the coastguard's red rescue vessel rounded the headland.

"You must be the owners of the luckiest dog in Cornwall." Paul's face was one huge grin as he jumped out of his jeep and led Molly to the door of the cottage.

The four family members threw themselves at their beloved pooch. Molly couldn't believe the overwhelming but welcome attention she was receiving.

"We pulled up in the boat and she jumped up straightaway, barking like a good 'un – think she must have been asleep."

"Well, that's one way of dealing with a crisis!" Charlotte regarded her dog with admiration while Molly gazed back at her dopily from beneath her fringe, her fluffy tail wagging furiously.

Alex hugged Molly more tightly than anyone else and buried her face in the dog's mane. "Molly, you big hairy twit."

"You all right?" asked Josh, coming up the path behind his father. Alex stood up and waved for him to join her. The two of them went to sit on the low dry-stone wall that enclosed the front garden, their heads close together, engrossed in conversation.

"She'll be fine."

"We can't thank you enough for everything you've done." Ed took Paul's hand and clasped it gratefully in thanks.

"Just another day for the coastguard, no 'arm done and all's ended well. I've earned me pint tonight, that's for sure."

"We owe you more than a pint," Charlotte said with feeling.

"I'll hold you to that!" Paul winked at her, then returned to his jeep, waiting patiently in the driver's seat while Josh and Alex swapped numbers. Then Josh jumped in and they drove off.

"I hope we see them again," said Alex, joining her mother on the sofa.

Charlotte put an arm around her daughter. "I'm sure we will, darling. We all want to come back here, even Molly does." Molly wagged her tail at the sound of her name.

Alex's face was buried in her hoodie and Charlotte could feel her shoulders shaking as more tears came. They'd all had a big fright today, so she wasn't surprised that Alex was still feeling fragile.

"I'm sorry I called you a shit and pushed you over," Alex told Sam

"What?" Sam looked up from his iPad,

where he'd been engrossed in his new obsession – Surf World. "Oh, that? Don't sweat it."

Alex smiled through her tears. "You are annoying, though."

Ed squeezed in next to his wife and daughter on the sofa. He gave Sam the head nod that said *Hop it*. Sam rolled his eyes at his dad's unsubtle hint, but for once restrained himself from making a clever remark.

"Come on, Molly – let's go bark at that cat that keeps hanging around for scraps outside." He bounded out of the back door, followed by the luckiest dog in Cornwall.

Alex continued to hold on to her mum, and Charlotte was reminded of when Alex was a baby, hating to be put down or held by anyone else. Those days were long ago, but it seemed her little girl still needed her mum after all.

"What is it, darling? Is there something else upsetting you?"

Alex didn't say anything but the question brought on a torrent of tears. Ed came and joined them on the sofa.

"You can tell me and your mum anything," he said encouragingly.

"Not anything!"

"Of course you can!" Charlotte squeezed her daughter's hand. "Is it something or someone at school? Is it about your new friend – Lily? She's not being horrid, is she?

At this there was a fresh bout of sobbing. "No, Lily's amazing, I... I..." Alex hesitated and her parents held their breath. "I... I've got feelings for her... I think I might be gay!"

Charlotte and Ed exchanged a brief wide-eyed look, then immediately rushed to reassure her with shushes, hugs and soothing words. "We love you no matter who you have feelings for," Charlotte said forcefully. "Don't we, Ed?"

"Absolutely! You mean the world to us and as long as you're happy, that's good enough for us."

"Really?"

"Really, really," they both said in unison.

Alex sniffed and wiped her nose on her cuff. "It's just that Josh... today... he was so nice. We exchanged numbers."

"Darling girl," said Charlotte, holding Alex to her tightly, "you're still working things out. You don't have to be anything yet. Growing up isn't easy and you'll take a few different turns along the way, but you'll sort it out eventually."

"You don't need to rush anything," agreed Ed.

"You remember Gloria – my best friend from university?" said Charlotte.

Alex nodded. "The one with those annoying twins: Gina and Angelina."

"And two annoying ex-husbands!" Charlotte laughed. "Well, when we were students, she was head of the Student Lesbian and Gay Alliance. She had a very handsome girlfriend called Mogs and they were inseparable."

Alex raised her eyebrows in astonishment.

"You can ask her next time you see her – Gloria's proud of her past. The thing is, people change – it's natural. If you care about someone, all you want is for them to be happy. Nothing else matters."

After a Chinese takeaway from Trevay, Alex had gone upstairs and Charlotte had tucked her in as if she were a little girl again. Then she came down and joined Ed on the sofa with a bottle of red wine.

"What a day!" Ed exhaled loudly. "Do you think she's gay?"

Charlotte thought about it for a moment. "Not sure. Maybe. Maybe not. Does it bother you?"

"Nope."

"Good."

They sipped their drinks in silence for a while. Then:

"Charlotte..."

"Ed..."

They spoke at the same time and an awkwardness descended over them.

Not again, Ed thought anxiously.

"There's something I need to tell you..." There was something ominous in her tone.

"It's about Henry, isn't it?"

Charlotte looked confused. "Well, yes – how did you know?"

All Ed's anxieties came bursting to the surface. "I just do," he blurted. "And I know what you're going to say – I saw the texts."

Charlotte was frowning. "What texts?"

"The ones that said, 'I love you...', 'I can't live without you.'"

He watched realisation dawn on her face, steeling himself for the bombshell to drop, for her to tell him that it was all over between them, that she was leaving. Instead she did the last thing he'd expected: she burst out laughing.

Lost for words, Ed looked at her aghast. How could she find anything amusing in this?

"Oh, Ed!" She tried to compose herself but couldn't stop the hilarity from bubbling over. "You're face is a picture!"

"Charlotte, I don't understand, what—"

She touched his face tenderly. "No, you don't understand, do you? After all your years in the business, I'd have thought you understood loveydom! Henry didn't mean me, he meant this." She took her phone from her pocket, scrolled through her gallery until she came to a series of photographs, and held it out for Ed to see.

Ed found himself looking at the most extraordinary theatre set – and it was clearly Charlotte's design, he'd recognise her style anywhere. "What is it?"

"The set of *The Lion, the Witch and the Wardrobe*. It's Henry's production and my set."

Ed knew his wife was supremely talented, but the innovative way that Charlotte had created an ice forest and integrated the vast wardrobe was extraordinary. He scrolled down: there was Badger's cosy underground set, the White Witch's palace, the stone table and Cair Paravel – it was breathtaking.

"I can't believe you've done all this." Though really he could.

"The production's been a huge success." She paused and took a deep breath. "Such a success that it's transferring to the West End. Henry wants me on board – he's asked me to go with him."

Ed didn't know what to say. Once again, he'd been struck dumb by Charlotte coming out with a momentous announcement that was going to change their lives.

He looked at his wife's face and saw in it the same girl who'd told him she was pregnant all those years ago. The woman who had given up everything for him and for their family.

A brief look of anguish crossed her face, but then it was gone and she set her lips in a thin line. "Of course, I know I can't go – Alex and Sam need one of us at home, and your job is too important to jeopardise. It was stupid for me to even consider it." She placed her glass on the table and made to stand up, as if the conversation was over. Ed pulled her back down and held her face in his hands. He was determined that this time he was going to get it right.

"Charlotte Appleby, my beautiful, talented wife. You've given me more than I could ever have expected and you've done the most amazing job of raising our children. I'd be a big wet puddle of worry and stress without you to keep me steady. I would literally go to the ends of the earth if you asked me to. So, if this is what you want, then we're going to make it happen."

Charlotte looked at him, incredulous. "Do you mean that?"

"Yes. I mean it more than anything I've said in my whole life. You've done your bit and now it's my turn. I'll tell Pen that she can promote Cassie. I can supervise from afar when necessary and do consultancy work, when I'm not too busy being a house-husband, that is."

"You mean you'll do all the cooking?"

"Yes. I doubt I can manage a prawn surprise, but I think the world will thank me for that, don't you?"

"Hey!" She gave him playful punch. "And all the cleaning?"

"I'll even wear a pinny."

"Why do I find that image strangely erotic?"

"Because you're a bit kinky?"

"I thought you'd forgotten."

"Impossible." And, before he could say anything else, Charlotte straddled her husband and started to remove his clothes.

Epilogue

Charlotte shook her children gently awake as the sun appeared below the horizon.

"We're here."

There was much moaning and groaning from the back.

"Mum, why are we doing this again? We already did it on the way." Sam stretched his arms and let out a huge yawn.

"I know, but this time we've got hot chocolate." She poured each of them half a beakerful from a brightly coloured Thermos. They all sipped at their cups for a few moments.

"Ready?" Ed asked as he collected up their cups. "No, it's freezing!"

"Then bring your blankets!"

He opened the door of the Volvo and the four of them headed along Stonehenge Avenue to the row of beech trees.

They sat down on a waterproof picnic blanket and settled themselves in. Molly gambolled around the field ahead, chasing the flocks of early-morning starlings as they started up their dawn chorus.

The rosy-coloured fingers of dawn crept above the horizon and the sun rose quickly into the morning sky, its golden rays illuminating the ancient triptychs of Stonehenge below them. They watched in silence.

"What do you think?" Charlotte asked the children, drinking in the sight. "This is the best time to see it. Are you more impressed this time?"

"Maybe," said Alex.

"I still think it's a bit small," Sam said, then added quickly, "But it's pretty cool, I suppose."

Ed looked at his wife ruefully. "Kids are always difficult to please – there's no such thing as perfection."

"No." But Charlotte wanted this moment to last for ever. The four of them, here together. Her family. "Except perhaps right here, right now." She leaned in to kiss her husband.

"Urgh! Get a room!" Sam and Alex shrieked, then ran away across the field, chasing after Molly, scattering the starlings as the sun rose over Salisbury Plain.

About the Author

Fern Britton is a highly acclaimed *Sunday Times* bestselling author of ten novels and other works. She started her career in TV current affair and news and become a household name in entrainment with hosting *This Morning* and *Read Steady Cook*. More recently she has presented *Watercolour Challenge* on Channel 5. Cornwall, where Fern lives with her family, is a recurring setting in her books.

Also by Fern Britton

Hidden Treasures Books

Hidden Treasures

A Seaside Affair

Standalone Novels

New Beginnings

The Holiday Home

A Good Catch

The Postcard

Coming Home

The Newcomer

Daughters of Cornwall

The Good Servant

Short Stories, Collections and Novellas

The Stolen Weekend

A Cornish Carol

The Beach Cabin

A Cornish Gift (collection)

The Great Cornish Getaway

Non-Fiction Books

Fern's Family Favourites

Winter Treats / Summer Delights
(with Susie Magasiner)

Fern: The Autobiography

The Older I Get...

Our Full Range of Dyslexic Friendly Books

Quick Reads

Anchor Point

At Midnight I Will Steal Your Soul

The Beach Cabin

Blood Toll

The Breath

The Clockwork Eyeball

Descendant

The Dust of the Red Rose Knight

The House on the Old Cliffs

Killer Instinct

The Necessary Arthur

Sharpe's Skirmish

Sherlock Holmes and the Four Kings of Sweden

Silver for Silence

Six Lights off Green Scar

Snow in the Desert

Stamp of a Criminal

Ultrasound Shadow

Classic Quick Reads

The Man Who Would Be King

Sherlock Holmes Collection

The Adventure of the Engineer's Thumb

The Adventure of the Speckled Band

The Boscombe Valley Mystery

The Man with the Twisted Lip

The Red-Headed League

A Scandal in Bohemia

Novels

The Wasp Factory

**More dyslexic friendly
titles coming soon...**

BOTH
PUBLISHING